DEAD SCARY
GHOST GUITAR

PENGUIN BOOKS

UK | USA | Canada | Ireland | Australia
India | New Zealand | South Africa | China

Penguin Random House Australia

Penguin Random House Australia is part of the Penguin Random House group of companies whose addresses can be found at global.penguinrandomhouse.com.

First published by Penguin, an imprint of Penguin Random House Australia Pty Ltd, in 2025

Cover and internal illustrations by Nahum Ziersch
Cover design by Rebecca King © Penguin Random House Australia Pty Ltd
Internal design by Caroline Lee © Penguin Random House Australia Pty Ltd
Typeset by Midland Typesetters, Australia

Printed and bound in Australia by Griffin Press, an accredited ISO AS/NZS 14001 Environmental Management Systems printer

NATIONAL LIBRARY OF AUSTRALIA
A catalogue record for this book is available from the National Library of Australia

MIX
Paper | Supporting responsible forestry
FSC www.fsc.org FSC® C018684

ISBN 978 1 76135 287 4 (Paperback)

We at Penguin Random House Australia acknowledge that Aboriginal and Torres Strait Islander peoples are the Traditional Custodians and the first storytellers of the lands on which we live and work. We honour Aboriginal and Torres Strait Islander peoples' continuous connection to Country, waters, skies and communities. We celebrate Aboriginal and Torres Strait Islander stories, traditions and living cultures; and we pay our respects to Elders past and present.

DEAD SCARY GHOST GUITAR

TJ DOOM

Illustrated by
Nahum Ziersch

PENGUIN BOOKS

A WARNING

Dear Reader,

The Dead Scary books aren't like any others.

They're twisted. They're spooky. They'll make you laugh and scream – sometimes at the same time. Most of all, they're exciting. Once you start, you'll never want to put them down.

But before you dive in, a warning.

Scary stories are strange things. The more you read, the more they stay with you. They creep into your mind, curl up in the shadows and whisper to you when the lights go out.

But you're brave. I can tell.

So go on, turn the page.

If you dare.

Sleep tight,
TJ DOOM

ABOUT THE AUTHOR

TJ DOOM lives off the grid in a crumbling mansion at the edge of a dark and windswept forest. Surrounded by creepy old portraits that appear to watch – and judge – the writer's every move, DOOM spends the long, haunted nights crafting sinister stories designed to do just one thing: mess with your head.

DOOM's tales are precision engineered for maximum dread. Some say that if DOOM's books are cracked open after midnight, the creatures inside won't just haunt your dreams, they'll crawl out of the pages and come looking for you.

TJ DOOM doesn't do interviews. Doesn't sign autographs. Won't even pose for a photo. Naturally, this has fuelled rumours that the writer is an ancient, blood-sucking vampire whose image can never be caught on camera.

Because DOOM is always uncontactable, this cannot be confirmed.

Or denied.

CHAPTER ONE

JAKE Jensen is not afraid of what's in his closet.

Yes, he knows that plenty of kids imagine that a monster lives there, especially at night when all is quiet and the slightest creak makes them think it's about to leap out and eat their face. But that's never freaked out Jake, not even when he was little.

Nope.

There's just one thing that creeps him out.

Gargoyles.

That's right, gargoyles.

How did they even become a thing?

Seriously, who thought it was a good idea to carve grotesque, human-sized creatures with razor-sharp fangs, flesh-ripping talons and bat-like wings into the side of buildings?

Well, apparently, the folks who built his school one hundred years ago, that's who.

As Jake strides towards the old music building, spookily named Nocturne House by some weirdo back in ancient times, he glances up at the towering, time-worn sandstone structure with the crouching gargoyle above its entrance – and involuntarily shivers. This building resembles a castle where an evil witch from a dark fairytale lives. The type who explodes into a flock of ravens when they need to make a quick getaway.

Nocturne House was the only building to survive the massive fire that tore through the school half a century ago, so it stands apart from the new buildings, coolly watching from the far corner of the manicured quadrangle. They are sleek and modern, all glistening steel and polished glass. They're too transparent to hold any secrets, while Nocturne House feels like it's hiding something dark and ominous.

Jake trots into the creepy building and moves down the draughty, marble-tiled hallway. He passes a poster calling for musical acts to sign up for the end-of-year Holiday Concert, then takes a left into the wood-panelled music room and grabs a seat. He might be only twelve years old, but a recent growth spurt means he's now taller than his classmates, which he does not hate.

He watches as all those shorter classmates pull out their homework.

Oh no!

The homework!

He forgot to do the homework.

Sitting to his left is his long-time bestie and neighbour, the very extra and extremely plucky Zoe Bianchi. He'd planned to do the homework once he got to school but got caught in a conversation with her about the meaning of a cryptic Taylor Nation Insta post.

Zoe is passionate about all matters Taylor Swift, so, as best mates do, Jake dutifully listened as she laid out her theories, such as there being a new album release on the horizon, or that someone dissed the singer/songwriter and was about to feel the sting of her retribution. They never did nail down the exact reason for the post and by the time the bell rang for first period it had been removed.

So, then Jake was going to do the homework at lunchtime. He even went to the library, where he would have done the homework if he had remembered he needed to do the homework. But instead, he spent the whole hour paging through the only really cool book in the entire place.

The one about vintage electric guitars.

Oh, how he wants an electric guitar. And it doesn't even need to be vintage. It just needs to be electric. While most kids like to make music on their computers, phones or tablets, Jake wants just one thing.

He wants to rock.

And start a rock band.

And fist bump his bandmates after nailing a killer song and say: 'And the rest is rock 'n' roll history.'

Actually, those are three things, but still, he needs an electric guitar to do them.

Jake's parental units (PUs) insist he buys his own electric guitar, because, he's sure, they want to delay the torture of listening to him practise for as long as they can. Unfortunately, the cheapest halfway decent one costs three hundred dollars.

Three hundred!

It's like the world is going out of its way to make it impossible for him to rock.

So, about two months ago, he decided to . . . wait for it . . . build his own guitar! That means, whenever he has a bit of spare cashola, he buys a second-hand part off the internet. He named the guitar Rockenstein because: 1) when it's complete he will use it to rock like no-one has ever rocked before, and 2) it's going to be stitched together from all kinds of second-hand parts, just like good old Frankenstein's monster.

The problem is, Rockenstein is nowhere close to being finished, because Jake is broke. Well, he does have some money, but it's the incredibly embarrassing sum of twenty-seven dollars and forty-three cents.

Sometimes he cuts lawns for fifteen bucks a go, but with homework and sport and chores, he barely has time to do that once a fortnight. He hopes his grandparents will make it rain at Christmas, but for now, he's learning to play on the weathered and ancient acoustic guitar he found during last year's council clean-up –

'Please hand in your homework.'

That's The Fossil entering the room. Talk about weathered and ancient. His actual name is Mister Harrington, but The Fossil makes a lot more sense because, seriously, someone needs to tell the guy to stop being so old. He must be a hundred and sixty-five. Or maybe just sixty-five. Who can tell the difference?

Anyway, The Fossil always collects homework from the front of the class. Jake stares at his blank homework sheet. He reckons he can complete it in the time it takes for The Fossil to reach where he sits at the back of the class. So, he pulls a pencil from his blazer pocket and reads the first question: Draw a treble clef on the staff.

Easy peasy.

He draws a treble clef.

No worries!

Second question: Draw a bass clef.

That's just like a treble clef except a bit different.

He draws the bass clef.

Done!

He's making good time.

Third question –

'Mister Jensen.'

Jake looks up and recoils as the craggy face of The Fossil looms in front of him. It seems The Fossil has started collecting the homework from the *back* of the class for the first time ever. 'I see you have failed to complete the homework on time.'

'Just putting the finishing touches on it now, sir.' At this school, students must call every teacher 'sir' or 'ma'am' as a sign of respect for their elders, which is especially appropriate for The Fossil, who is the most elderly of them all.

'And why didn't you do it before now?'

'It was my dog, sir.'

'Are you saying your dog ate your homework?'

'No, sir. I don't have a dog, and that made me sad so I didn't feel like doing any homework.'

The other students laugh as The Fossil stares at Jake. 'Mister Jensen, that might be your worst excuse yet.'

'But it almost made you smile.'

'No. No it didn't.' The Fossil whips the paper away from Jake with knobbly fingers so freaky they'd make Nosferatu jealous. 'You had plenty of time to finish this.' Then, he turns to the class and asks, 'What do I always say?'

The class all answer in a dull drone: 'If you can't be on time, be early.'

'Exactly. And you are neither, Mister Jensen. You are, in fact, late.' The Fossil continues collecting the papers.

'Oh, come on, you old fossil, give me a break.'

The whole class hear this and go 'Ooohhh' as The Fossil turns and looks back at Jake.

Jake winces. 'Did I say that out loud?'

The Fossil nods. 'Yes. Yes, you did.'

Jake tries to walk it back. 'Then, may I also say that I fully and unreservedly apologise for that indiscretion, sir.'

The Fossil nods. 'Thank you, Mister Jensen. I do appreciate that –'

Jake sighs a deep sigh of relief.

Yes! Catastrophe averted!

'– and see me after class to start your week of detention.'

The whole class go 'Ooohhh' again.

Jake can't believe his ears. 'But sir –'

The Fossil raises a finger to silence him. 'If you want to make it two weeks, then please, keep talking.'

Jake opens his mouth to keep talking then feels a sharp sting as Zoe kicks him in the shin. He glances over and she shakes her head. Jake promptly shuts his mouth.

He's furious with himself.

Not only will his PUs get an email announcing his five (yes, five!) days of detention, but now, after slogging his way through another brutal week of school, he's stuck staying late on a Friday (a Friday!) instead of kicking off the weekend with a breezy, sun-soaked summer afternoon, which is his favourite kind of afternoon.

So, for the rest of the class he's a bit of a sulky lala, truth be told. It takes forever before the bell rings and all the students file out, except for Jake. He remains seated and watches The Fossil clean the chalkboard. Yes, he's such an antique he prefers to use that instead of a whiteboard.

The Fossil finally turns to his remaining student, his weary face etched with more lines than a crumpled road map. His deep-set eyes carry the weight of decades of dealing with uppity students (like Jake) while his wiry frame sags under a heavy tweed jacket. Even his bow tie, slightly askew, looks like it knows he's a bad hang.

'So,' The Fossil eventually says after the longest time, 'you'll be compiling a list of everything that's in the attic.'

Jake grins. That doesn't sound so bad. 'That doesn't sound so bad.'

'Then you'll box it all up so it can be put in long-term storage.'

Jake grimaces. He spoke too soon. 'I spoke too soon.'

The Fossil nods. 'Yes, you did. The room has been used as a dumping ground for, well, as long as I can remember, so it's packed full of junk. It's going to take you a while. But that's okay. You have plenty of time. A whole week, in fact.'

The Fossil pulls his sad-sack mouth into the shape of a grin then passes Jake a stack of flat-packed cardboard boxes along with a paper pad and a pen. 'I cannot tell you how excited I am that I don't have to do it.'

Jake studies the supplies glumly. 'Wow, this is a *ton* of work.'

'Then you'll have to dig deep, won't you?' The Fossil glances at his watch and frowns. 'I have to get going. Work on the list until five and we'll see how far you've got on Monday.'

'No, we'll see how far *you've* got on Monday.' Of course this doesn't make any sense, but saying it to himself as he trudges up the marble steps on his way to the attic makes Jake feel a little better. With the supplies in hand, he reaches the third floor and passes a music room where some unfortunate kid is playing the *Titanic* theme on a recorder. Amazingly, it sounds even more out-of-tune than that version he's heard on a bajillion TikToks.

Jake searches for the steps up to the attic but quickly realises the only access is a tight, wrought-iron spiral staircase that perfectly matches the eerie vibe of this creepy old building. The higher he goes, the dimmer it gets as the discordant strains of the *Titanic* theme fade into the depths below like a haunted, distant echo.

With each step the stairwell creaks under his weight, the metal groaning like it hasn't been used in years. Dust clings to the handrail and cobwebs brush his face as he ascends. Then a strange hush settles over everything, like the building is listening. Jake swallows hard and keeps moving, trying not to imagine what might be waiting for him at the end of this climb.

When Jake reaches the top of the staircase it's so dark he can't see where the light switch is, or if there even is a light switch. Then he feels a chill and the skin on his arms goes goosebumpy. He thought the outside of this building was the spookiest thing at this school but this, right here, gives it a good run for its money.

He fishes his phone out of his back pocket and presses on the flashlight. The beam cuts through the suffocating darkness ahead of him –

A grotesque, snarling face lurches towards him, its twisted mouth curled into a vicious grin, its razor-sharp teeth and hollow eyes glinting in the light.

With a gasp, Jake stumbles backwards and falls . . .

CHAPTER TWO

WHUMP!

Jake lands hard – then realises the monstrous face isn't lurching towards him. It is, in fact, chiselled into the wooden door that stands in front of him.

Why would anyone put that there?!

The door must have been carved by the same weirdo who designed the creepy gargoyle out front. Its grin is wide and wicked, with jagged teeth and staring eyes that seem to follow you. It's as if the thing was conjured from a nightmare and feels wildly over-the-top for a school, even one built over a hundred years ago. Simply, it makes Jake's skin crawl.

Jake shakes off the scare, then stands and takes a deep breath. He grips the doorknob and twists it open and, with a quick push and a loud creak of hinges, steps into the attic.

The smell punches him in the face. This place has the sharp aroma of his grandfather's study, which is a combination of dust and old newspapers (which is where people used to get their news before the internet). It's not the worst smell in the world, if he's being honest.

Light streams through two windows at either end of the large room and illuminates how crammed full of stuff it is. Make that old stuff. Stacks of papers, amplifiers, a drum kit, speakers, tangled clumps of cables, microphones and piles of sheet music. And everything is covered in a thick layer of dust, which, he was recently grossed out to learn, is pretty much all made up of dead human skin cells.

So, where to start? First, Jake opens the windows to let in some fresh air, then finds a faded plastic chair and takes a seat. He places the pad and pen on his knees, and focuses on the stack of papers in front of him.

The pen instantly rolls off the pad and hits the floor. He bends to pick it up – and sees something, partially hidden behind a stack of sheet music that's pushed deep under a rickety cupboard on the other side of the room. It's a long, thin and, yes, dusty old case for a musical instrument.

Could it be a guitar?

Gee, Jake hopes so.

Imagine if it *was* an electric guitar. A real, genuine electric guitar!

Intrigued, he rushes over and drags it from under the cupboard. It's heavy, so it's definitely not empty. The case is a perfect rectangle, its black finish worn and faded. Jake works the tarnished latches and they snap open with a sharp clack.

He's sure this whole thing is going to end up being a huge disappointment. It'll be a ginormous bassoon or something. So, he opens the lid without great expectations and –

Inside is no bassoon.

No, it's the most beautiful vintage electric guitar Jake has ever seen, though he's never actually seen one for real, just in books, or on the internet.

It sends a surge of emotion through him so raw and powerful that his eyes well up. It's a primal feeling of joy he's never known before, as if the very sight of the instrument has awakened something buried deep within his soul.

He knows exactly what kind of guitar it is.

A Fender Telecaster.

Or, as professional guitarists call it, a 'Tele'. And he's pretty sure the name of the colour is Daphne Blue, which looks like the sky on the clearest, happiest day of your life.

Suddenly, getting detention is totally worth it. Jake never dreamed he'd get the chance to see a guitar this epic, let alone pick it up and hold it in his hands, which he does right now. It's heavy and feels important, like it's imbued with the spirit of all who rocked it before. He turns it over to look at the serial number on the neck plate – and stops dead.

It's been burned.

Scorched shadows crawl across the wood, fractured patches of that gorgeous Daphne Blue barely visible beneath the blackened scars. It's as if the guitar has been through something unspeakable, its dark history hidden in the bubbled, charred paint.

Jake wonders if this damage was done on purpose. He's never understood why some guitarists destroy their instruments as part of the show. He's seen it on YouTube and can't imagine a situation in which he would do that.

Jake checks the serial number that's stamped into the tarnished neck plate and sees that this guitar was built in 1962.

1962!

Why would someone leave it here, hidden under this cupboard? It's so rare and valuable, even with the burn marks (which only make it more interesting to Jake). But more than that, you can actually play music with it. Intense, loud rock music. Or rhythmic, funky rock music. Why wouldn't you want to use it to do that *all the time*?

Jake thinks that's what he should do right now. After all, he's meant to catalogue everything that's in this attic and he couldn't very well say the guitar was in working order, or not, without playing it, could he?

No, he could not. So, he looks around and sees an old amplifier with the word 'Marshall' written on the front grill. He turns it on, plugs the guitar into it then notices a single, gold guitar pick at the bottom of the case. It's shaped like a strawberry, with a wide end tapering to a sharp, blade-like point. He grabs it with his right hand and realises it's made of metal and has a nice weight to it. Then he takes the neck of the guitar in his left hand, lets his fingers find the strings and raises the pick high.

If Jake knew that playing one chord on this guitar would plunge him into a world of spine-chilling horror the likes of which a twelve-year-old had never faced before, would he still do it?

Probably.

That's how much he wants to play this guitar.

But Jake doesn't know any of that, so he swings the pick down and perfectly strikes the guitar strings to create the very musical chord of E minor 9, which he learned off YouTube two weeks ago. It's by far Jake's favourite chord at the moment.

The sound blasts out of the amplifier and reverberates across the attic with such intensity that it's like Jake can almost see ripples in the air.

Then he *can* see ripples in the air.

Three of them.

'What the –?' For a split-second Jake thinks his eyes are playing tricks on him, then the ripples become larger until they're so big they stretch from the ceiling to the floor and fill the entire room.

The ripples twist and spiral, spinning faster and faster until they stretch into a long, shimmering tunnel. From its depths blasts a piercing beam of light that floods the attic as the air crackles and churns, whipping into a cyclone that roars in Jake's ears and sweeps all the loose papers into a swirling chaos. He feels the air press against him, pull at his clothes, rattle the bones in his chest.

Jake's hands tremble, sweat slicking his palms as the storm howls around him. He should run from here, get to a safe place, and yet, beneath his fear, something else stirs – an intrepid curiosity. He can't

look away from the impossible sight before him. So, he stays put.

'What. Is. Happening?' His words hang in the air, trembling like the attic itself, as if daring the universe with the question.

Then he gets the answer.

Three glowing, translucent apparitions emerge from the swirling tunnel, their forms like burning embers wreathed in smoke.

Jake's breath catches in his throat as they glide forward, impossibly real and yet undeniably there. The hairs on his arms stand rigid as shock and horror collide.

Then the apparitions' glowing eyes lock on Jake. They sweep towards him, their shimmering forms radiating an otherworldly presence that makes him wonder – is this it?

Is this the end?

Is this how he dies?

CHAPTER THREE

JAKE instinctively steps back as the apparitions float across the room, their feet never touching the floor.

It's almost like they're ghosts.

No. That can't be.

Because ghosts aren't real.

But that's exactly what they look like.

Ghosts.

Not the 'cut out the eye holes of Grandma's old sheet and drape it over your head' version that you might use as a no-budget Halloween costume, but more the 'horrifying spirit from the netherworld that has come to steal your soul' type.

In a flash, the swirling tunnel behind the apparitions dissipates and the roaring windstorm fades away. The glowing apparitions begin to shimmer and shift, solidifying into something shockingly real.

Jake stands frozen, his breath caught in his throat, as pure, undiluted panic surges through him. His gut turns with a single, crushing realisation – he should have run the second he had the chance instead of being so intrepidly curious.

Well, it's too late now.

The apparitions twist and contort as the smoke that clings to them pulses and shifts.

Jake takes another step back, his every instinct bracing for something unspeakable.

Something monstrous.

Something terrible.

Then Jake blinks.

And three teenagers stand before him.

They look like they've just stepped off a school bus, not flown out of a supernatural abyss.

Yep. Two guys and a girl stand in front of him. Jake stares at them, totally freaked. He should still turn and run. What if they attack?! In fact, why isn't he running right now?

Because they don't attack.

But they do smile.

At him.

The kids look about fifteen years old. They have weird hair and wear tight jeans with wide bottoms ('bell-bottoms' Jake's mum calls them) and strange T-shirts in a collection of pretty blah colours.

The tall boy with long red hair sports a mustard yellow T-shirt with AC/DC written on it. Jake knows they're a famous old Aussie rock band and he loves a song of theirs called 'Jailbreak', which his grandad once played to him. It has an amazing guitar riff, so Jake streams it all the time.

The girl has long brown hair and wears a faded blue T-shirt with Led Zeppelin written on it. They're another ancient band, and Jake practises a song of theirs called 'Stairway to Heaven' a lot. It's considered to be a classic rock ballad.

And the blond guy in the middle has an off-white T-shirt on with Queen emblazoned across it. Well, everybody knows that band. 'Bohemian Rhapsody' is one of Jake's favourite songs and he saw a movie about them on Netflix a while back with his mum, who also loves them.

The blond guy in the Queen T-shirt is the first to speak. 'Well, that took long enough.'

This bloke has so much rizz and is so effortlessly cool that the fear Jake was feeling instantly evaporates. 'What took a while?'

'For someone to play my guitar.'

Jake holds up the Telecaster. 'This is yours?'

'Yep, and you're the first one to play it in – what year is this?'

'2025.'

The teens are visibly shocked by the number and mutter: 'Oh my,' 'Wow-wee,' and 'That can't be right.'

'It's absolutely right,' Jakes tells them. 'So, who are you?'

The blond guy shakes off his surprise. 'Sorry, where are my manners? I'm Ricky. Vocals and guitar.' He points at the girl. 'That's JoBeth. Bass.' Then he points at the redhead. 'And that's Timbo. Drums. We're Ricky & the Blue Jeans.'

'So, you're a band who are also – ghosts?' Jake can't believe he's asking the question.

The teens nod in unison.

Jake blinks, his brain scrambling to catch up. 'So, that means ghosts are an actual thing?' It's more a statement than a question.

The synchronised nods come again.

Jake takes a moment to process this as Ricky asks: 'And who might you be?'

'Oh. Uh, Jake. I'm Jake. My name's Jake.' He stumbles over the words, still reeling from the whirlwind of recent events. 'So, why are you here?'

'You summoned us by playing my Telecaster. Nice strum, by the way.' Ricky is impressed. 'Very musical.'

'Thank you, but I'm stuck on the part where you said I "summoned" you.' Jake makes air quotes with his fingers when he says 'summoned'. '"Summoned" from where?'

Timbo answers, his voice serious. 'Limbo. The place between this world and the afterlife. We've been stuck there for fifty years. Since December 6th, 1975.'

Jake is astounded. 'That's a really long time ago. Why are you there?'

The three teens look at each other, then Ricky speaks: 'Because the last time we played together we completed our first two songs but didn't finish the third.'

Jake nods, but he's confused. 'And why didn't you finish the third?'

'Because we died.'

'Oh! Right. Of course. That's why you're ghosts. Sorry. So, what happened?'

Timbo explains. 'It was the Christmas Concert, just before the summer break. A Saturday night. We'd been practising for weeks and sounded great. After the first and second songs we had the audience in the palm of our hand, so we wanted to bring it home strong with "One and Only", which was our best song. The problem was, we were so in the zone that we didn't realise what was happening behind us.'

Jake is on the edge of his seat. 'What was happening behind us?'

Ricky shakes his head. 'The Assembly Hall's fuse box short-circuited and caught fire.'

'So, you ran straight out of there and – oh no.' Mortified, Jake suddenly remembers the charred back of the guitar hanging around his neck. 'That's when you, you, you –'

'Hit the final snooze button.' Ricky fills in the blanks. 'Anyway, the place instantly went up in flames because everything in the seventies was highly flammable.'

'Including the students.' Timbo laughs at his own joke, then abruptly stops. 'Sorry, that was dark.'

'By the time we understood something was wrong, it was too late. We were trapped.'

Jake is genuinely horrified to hear this. 'I'm so sorry that happened to you.' Then he's confused. 'Why, exactly, are you telling me this?'

Ricky answers. 'We need your help to escape Limbo so we can move on to the afterlife.'

Jake is flabbergasted. 'Um. Okay. But how?'

'It'll happen if we can play our whole set of songs but actually complete the third one.'

'How do you know that will work?'

JoBeth explains. 'As soon as you arrive in Limbo, you know why you're there and what you have to do to move on. I don't know how, but you just know.'

'Well,' says Jake excitedly, 'let's do it now.'

Timbo shakes his head. 'It's not that easy. It has to be in front of the whole school, like it was back in 1975.'

'Right.' Jake thinks about that, then has a thought. 'The Holiday Concert is tomorrow night. Would that work?'

The band love the idea. 'That'd be a gas. You'll have to find our rhythm guitarist to play with us, though. His name is – is . . .'

For the life of him, Timbo can't remember the name, so after a moment JoBeth helps him out. 'JF Waronika.'

'That's it! JF Waronika.'

'Okay. Cool.' Jake nods. 'But what if I can't find this JF Waronika guy? Or what if I can and he freaks out when I tell him?'

'Then someone will need to take his place.'

'I could do it!' Jake blurts it out, then attempts to play it cool. 'I mean, if you want. I'm pretty good at guitar.' Jake knows pretty good is a bit of a stretch, but he wants to play in a band so bad he's willing to tell a fib to make it happen.

Ricky takes this in with a smile. 'We'll see, but try to find JF. He wrote our music and we've forgotten the lyrics to our last song. It's called "One and Only".'

Jake is surprised. 'You forgot your own song?'

Ricky nods. 'After you've been in Limbo for a while you still remember important things, like your name and who you were and what happened in your life, but little details start to go, like the lyrics to a song you sang a few times fifty years ago.'

Timbo's face darkens as he nods. 'That's why we have to move on to the afterlife. It's only a matter of time before we forget everything. And when that happens, we become one of . . . them.' He tries to keep his tone steady, but the word drips with dread.

Jake catches the weight of what Timbo is saying. 'And who, exactly, are "them"?'

Ricky answers coolly. 'Some call them "wandering spirits". Others say "lost souls". But we call them what they really are – phantom demons.'

Jake tries to make light of it. 'Phantom demons? Seriously? Two scary names? That seems like overkill.'

JoBeth shakes her head. 'It's not. They are heinous. They run Limbo and don't want us, or anyone, to escape it. They need us to forget, because when we do, we become one of them. And the more of them there are, the more powerful they become.'

Jake sucks in a sharp breath, his face tightening into a grimace. 'Well, that sounds bad.'

Ricky's grin is cold and humourless. 'And that's not even the worst part.'

'There's a worse part?'

Timbo nods. 'Whenever the portal between Limbo and the real world opens, they can pass through, unseen.'

Jake's eyes widen at this information. 'You mean, like the portal you guys just came through?'

JoBeth nods. 'Exactly.'

Jake forces a weak laugh. 'Well, let's just hope that never happens.'

As the words leave his mouth, the band recoils. Their features twist with raw terror as their eyes lock onto something behind Jake, sending a spike of icy dread down his spine. 'It's already happened, hasn't it?'

The band nods in horrified unison.

'And it's right behind me.'

Another horrified nod from the teen ghosts.

Jake doesn't want to turn around, doesn't want to see what's lurking there. Because if actual ghosts are afraid of it, then whatever it is must be something out of a nightmare . . .

CHAPTER FOUR

JAKE swallows hard, his heart pounding as he realises there's no use stalling. Whatever nightmare the phantom demon has conjured behind him, he's going to have to deal with it at some point. So, he takes a breath to brace himself, then turns around –

On the other side of the room, he sees a churning mass of black smoke and shifting shadows that appears to be alive, its form constantly curling and turning and collapsing on itself, never fully solid, yet terrifyingly real. Tendrils of shadow and smoke reach out from its core, coiling and snapping like vipers.

QUEEN

It's not just fear but a wave of suffocating, bone-deep terror that washes over Jake. He knows with absolute certainty that this moment will etch itself into his mind forever, lurking in the dark corners of his memory, ready to haunt him for the rest of his life.

Bam!

The sharpest, most revolting smell Jake has ever encountered smacks him across the face like a rotting fish. 'Oh my god. What is *that*?!' His hand flies up to cover his nose. 'It's foul!'

'It's the stench of the phantom demon,' Timbo stammers, his voice trembling with terror.

'That's not what Limbo smells like, is it?'

The band all answer in the affirmative.

'No wonder you want to leave.'

The air around the phantom demon suddenly becomes heavy, suffused with a malevolent energy that Jake can feel prick against his skin. His chest tightens with another wave of that primal terror. It isn't just in his mind either, but it feels like it's clawing at his insides, warning him with every instinct that whatever this thing is, it's not only dangerous but deeply, deeply wrong.

Then the creature shifts and, for a fleeting moment, something within it stares at Jake with blazing eyes filled with a malice so intense that it drills into his very soul. His hands shake as he steps back, realising he's face-to-face with a horror beyond anything he thought existed. Then it sweeps silently across the room, flies through the open door and is gone. Fortunately, it takes the horrendous smell with it.

Jake's voice wavers as he turns to the band. 'Where did it go?'

Ricky's face is grim. 'To rest and gain power.'

JoBeth's eyes darken. 'The longer it stays in the world of the living, the stronger it becomes.'

A cold shiver races down Jake's spine. 'And why, exactly, does it need to be strong?'

'So it can bring inanimate objects to life.'

Jake's breath catches. 'And why would it need to do that?'

Timbo's tone is foreboding. 'To stop you from helping us.'

Jake's stomach clenches. 'This is kind of freaking me out, guys.'

'It should.' Ricky's eyes lock on Jake. 'It will do anything to stop you. Anything. So, when it returns, you must be ready.'

'Are my family or friends in danger?'

'Only if they help you help us.'

None of this is news Jake was hoping to hear.

Ricky sees it and gives him an out. 'It will be dangerous, so you're not obligated to help us if you don't want to.'

The weight of the situation presses down on Jake but then he realises – who else will help them, if not him? 'Of course I'll help. I strummed the guitar, so I'm your guy. I'm just taking a moment to get used to the whole smokey-shadow-monster-wants-to-kill-me thing.' Jake rubs his face and takes a deep breath, which seems to steady his nerves a little. 'Okay, so tell me about this JF fella. How do I find him?'

'He used to write his lyrics in a little leather notebook. I remember that much,' volunteers JoBeth.

‘And he loved Led Zeppelin but couldn’t stand “Stairway to Heaven”,’ offers Ricky.

‘Not sure any of that will help me locate him.’

‘He used to write our songs up here, because this is where we rehearsed.’ JoBeth looks around the attic with a grimace. ‘It was a lot nicer back then. His notebook might be here somewhere.’

Jake waits for more information but nothing else comes. ‘That’s it? That’s *all* you’ve got?’

The band nods. That’s all they’ve got.

‘That’s a little disappointing, guys.’

Ricky agrees. ‘I know. It blows. I mean, we remember him, but we just can’t *remember* him.’

‘Like where he lived?’

The band shake their heads.

‘Or his phone number?’

The ghost teens shake their heads again as the air behind them begins to ripple like before. Then the ripples twist and contort, forming that spinning, shimmering tunnel. A piercing light bursts through it, flooding the attic with the same eerie golden glow as the air roils into a swirling cyclone.

Jake gestures to the churning tunnel and raises his voice over the windstorm: 'Does that mean you're leaving now?'

Ricky nods. 'We can only stay for so long. But you can call on us again. Just strum the guitar. But be careful. You only get two more goes at it.'

'Two? Seriously? Why?'

JoBeth shrugs, her expression apologetic. 'We don't make the rules. And when you open the portal, know that the phantom demon will be drawn to it. Whatever happens, never, *ever* let it drag you inside.'

Jake is deeply concerned. 'Why?'

'Because then you'll end up in Limbo too.'

The words hit Jake like a slap, but before he can say anything the ghost teens start to shimmer and shift, their forms dissolving back into translucent apparitions. Then the swirling tunnel draws them in, their glowing figures disappearing one by one into its depths before it collapses on itself and vanishes like it was never there. In the same moment, the howling gale ceases and the papers caught in its frenzy drift softly to the floor, settling in an uneasy silence.

Jake stands in the middle of the attic, which is now even messier than when he first walked in. But the clutter around him is the least of his concerns. He now has a mission with three parts:

One: Uncover the band's forgotten song.

Two: Track down their rhythm guitarist, JF Waronika.

Three: Ensure Ricky & the Blue Jeans can perform at the Holiday Concert, an event overseen by The Fossil himself, who is the school's ancient guardian of all things musical.

The kicker? The phantom demon, a malevolent force from Limbo, is out there, somewhere, gaining power, waiting for the perfect moment to strike. Jake swallows hard, knowing his quest won't just be difficult, it might be deadly as well.

He starts the mission by pulling out his phone, swiping open his school's app and snagging the one remaining free slot in the Holiday Concert's line-up. The band will play last.

The app prompts him to include the band's name, but Jake isn't sure what to put. Ricky & the Blue Jeans? That might be a little weird if anyone remembers what happened back in the day. So, instead, he writes RBJ, which sounds like a modern take on the old name, then lists himself as the band's contact.

With that done, Jake thinks that if there's a chance JF's lyric notebook is somewhere within this cluttered attic, he has to look for it. There's only one problem. There's *so much* stuff in this room he's going to need someone to help him sort through it. So he pulls out his phone to message Zoe. He's tempted to tell her what just happened with the ghosts and the phantom demon and everything, then decides against it. To actually talk about it seems like a giant leap into Crazytown, population: Jake. There's no reason to drag her into it. So, he sends her a text that just says she should come up and check out the attic.

Three minutes later, the creepy door with the spooky carvings swings open and Zoe strides in, a backpack with a water bottle stuck in its side pocket slung over her shoulder, AirPods in her ears and school tie loose around her neck.

Zoe hates that they have to wear a school uniform more than anyone Jake knows. In fact, it annoys her to the point that she's willing to make a silent protest by wearing her tie loose and top button undone every single day, knowing full well that she risks a Saturday detention for it. She has yet to land one and Jake can only guess that the teachers like her so much they don't have the heart to punish her. He understands that. He likes her that much too. She's his sister from another mother.

'Why did the banana go to the doctor?' Zoe always likes to enter a room with a joke. She thinks it sets an upbeat tone.

'Why?'

'Because it wasn't peeling very well.'

Jake chuckles. Around here, the golden rule is simple: the cornier the joke, the funnier it is.

'You should have warned me about the gargoyle on the door,' she says. 'That thing is terrifying.'

Jake nods in agreement. 'How you doing, Z-dog?'

Zoe looks at Jake suspiciously. 'Don't Z-dog me.'

'What?' Jake acts all innocent.

'You only call me Z-dog when you want my help with something.'

Jake keeps up the innocent act. 'Really? That doesn't sound like me.'

'It sounds *exactly* like you. What do you want?'

'Nothing. Can't I be happy to see my friend and neighbour?'

These two have lived next door to each other since they were three years old.

Zoe ain't buying it. 'I'm not helping with whatever he's making you do up here.'

'I didn't expect you to.'

'You absolutely did.'

Jake grins. 'I absolutely did.'

'Exactly. You got yourself into this, you can get yourself out. You called him an *old fossil* for goodness sake.'

'Well, he *is* an old fossil.'

'And you said it to his face.'

'It slipped out.'

She is dubious but accepts it with a nod, then looks around the room. 'So, what's the old fossil got you doing up here, anyway?'

'I have to catalogue then pack up everything in this room. In a week.'

Zoe laughs out loud. 'There's no way on Earth you'll get that done.'

'Sure I will, with your help –'

'I told you, that's not happening. I have better things to do.' She turns on her heel and heads for the door.

She almost makes it.

'We can listen to Taylor the whole time.' He goes big, knowing it's the only way to change her mind.

Zoe stops walking and looks at Jake. 'Can I explain what each song means and who it's about after we listen to it?'

Jake pulls in a deep, unsteady breath. He enjoys the vocal stylings and undeniable songwriting abilities of T-Swizzle, but he is resistant to this request because Zoe has already explained every single Taylor Swift song to him at some point in their relationship. At least *three* times. 'Absolutely.'

'Yay!' Zoe is pumped.

'Yay!' Jake pretends to be pumped.

Zoe pulls out a barrel-shaped Bluetooth speaker from her backpack and sets it up on a stack of old periodicals about teaching music. Just quietly, Zoe is a killer keyboardist, like seriously good, but for some reason she hates playing in front of people. He wants to start a band with her but she keeps shutting him down. He figures she's just a bit shy.

'There is one other thing.'

Zoe turns to Jake. 'What is it?'

'We need to find an old, leather-bound notebook –'

'Like this?' Zoe holds up an old, leather-bound notebook.

Jake is stunned. 'What?! Where was that?'

'Sitting right here.' She points at the stack of old magazines in front of her.

Jake holds his breath. 'Is it written by JF Waronika?'

Zoe points at the name printed inside the cover: *JF Waronika*.

Jake is amazed. 'Does it have the lyrics to a song called "One and Only" in it?'

Zoe flips through it, stops at a page. 'Yep.'

She then passes the notebook to Jake. It has that song in it all right, and includes handwritten music, notations and lyrics for the first two pages at least. Unfortunately, by the third page everything is badly faded, like it's been left open in the sun for a few decades. 'Dang,' he says, 'one of the verses is missing.'

'Why is that a big deal? Does The Fossil need it for –'

Boom. Boom. Boom.

Zoe is cut off by the steady, resonant beat of a kick drum. Jake knows it's the big one in a drum kit that sits on the floor, is played with a foot-pedal and is responsible for the deep, punchy thud that is the foundation of every rock song.

It's weird, though.

The sound is loud.

Like, *very* loud.

Boom. Boom. Boom.

It's so loud that it sounds like it's coming from right behind them. Puzzled, Jake looks back – and, quite simply, sees one of the creepiest things he's ever laid eyes on.

It rises from the shadows near the window Jake left open at the far end of the attic – slow, deliberate and wholly unnatural. Then it steps forward, emerging from the darkness, its form swaying in time with the pounding beat of the kick drum.

Boom. Boom. Boom.

The rhythm shakes the floorboards.

Then Zoe turns and sees it too – and recoils in horror. 'What the actual heck?!'

CHAPTER FIVE

IT'S ten feet tall and looks like the Incredible Hulk, if the Incredible Hulk were constructed from the individual parts of a drum kit.

Its feet are made from crash cymbals.

Its legs are built from tom drums.

Its mid-section is one, large kick drum.

Its arms are built from bongos.

Its hands are hi-hat cymbals.

And its head is a snare drum.

Boom. Boom. Boom.

The kick drum's tempo increases as the Drum Hulk moves towards Jake and Zoe. Its cymbal feet crash into the floor and are then instantly silenced by its weight.

Zoe glances at Jake. 'What is that?'

'I'll tell you as soon as we get out of here.'

They turn and sprint for the exit. On their way, Zoe grabs her backpack and throws it over her shoulders. They blast through the door, swing down the spiral staircase and reach the third floor. They are quick, but the Drum Hulk is quicker. In a flash it's right behind them as they launch down the marble steps.

Zoe thinks fast, grabs the bottle from the side of her backpack and squirts water onto the top step.

Boom. Boom. Boom.

The Drum Hulk's cymbal feet slip on the wet marble and it loses its balance. *Crunch!* It slams onto the steps and explodes into its individual parts. *Boom! Thunk! Smash!* The drums and cymbals blast into Jake and Zoe and knock them down like a pair of bowling pins.

As they scramble to their feet, the phantom demon twists and churns before them, a mass of writhing smoke and shifting shadow, stretching and pulsing like it's alive and angry. Then, with

a jarring clatter, it seizes all the pieces of the drum kit and reassembles itself into the Drum Hulk.

Zoe watches it, astonished, her voice barely a whisper: 'How is this possible?' Then the fetid, acrid stench slaps her in the face. She recoils, covering her nose. 'And what is that smell?!'

'It's called the phantom demon. And that's how it smells.'

'It's making my eyes water,' she says as she rubs at them. 'How do you know this?'

Jake realises there's no way to say it that doesn't sounds cray-cray. 'This afternoon, in the attic, I accidentally summoned three teen ghosts from 1975. They told me.'

Zoe stops rubbing her eyes and glares at him. 'You met three teen ghosts from the mid-seventies and didn't tell me?'

'I figured you'd think I was delulu.'

'Can't argue with that.' Their eyes flick to the Drum Hulk as it completes its grotesque reassembly and its kick drum heartbeat thunders back to life.

Boom. Boom. Boom.

Without saying a word, Jake and Zoe turn and bolt for the next set of stairs. They're almost there when Zoe has a better idea and points: 'The elevator!'

The elevator is the distance of a basketball court away and its doors are wide open.

Behind them, the Drum Hulk barrels forward, its massive form moving with ungainly but shocking speed, each thunderous step quickly closing the distance to Jake and Zoe.

Thirty metres, twenty metres, ten metres . . .

Hearts pounding, Jake and Zoe run for the elevator as hard as they can – then dive inside. Zoe swings around and jams her thumb against the Door Close button.

The doors don't close.

Boom. Boom. Boom.

They watch the Drum Hulk sprint towards them, its razor-sharp cymbal hands glinting in the light.

Zoe presses the button again. 'Come on!'

Still nothing.

Boom. Boom. Boom.

The Drum Hulk looms before them!

Then the elevator doors finally decide to close.

But they take *forever.*

Boom. Boom. Boom.

The Drum Hulk is right there!

Jake and Zoe recoil –

Thunk! The doors slam shut, cutting off the Drum Hulk with a split-second to spare. For a breathless moment, the world is silent. Then a petrified Zoe turns to Jake, a shaky grin forming. 'Doesn't get much closer than that –'

Screech. Metal grinds on metal as two cymbals wedge themselves through the gap between the elevator doors and start to wrench them apart.

Jake jams his thumb on the button that says G for Ground. The elevator descends and the cymbals quickly rise in the gap until they slam into the roof – then are pulled out and disappear from view.

Jake and Zoe stand in shocked silence, processing what just happened. After a beat,

Zoe is the first to break the silence: 'I love the seventies. Were the ghosts wearing bell-bottoms?'

Jake nods. 'Actually, they were.'

Ding! The lift reaches the ground floor. Jake and Zoe brace themselves, muscles tensed, ready for anything. The doors slide open –

No sign of the Drum Hulk.

They exhale sharply as relief washes over them. But they don't waste time. They bolt. Out of Nocturne House and straight to Jake's locker. He grabs his backpack and then they're running again, hearts hammering, legs burning, until they reach their parked bikes.

They jump on and take off, swerve out of the school and pedal for their homes like their lives depend on it. Because maybe they do.

As they go, they keep glancing behind them, expecting to see the Drum Hulk following. They don't, but that doesn't stop them from riding as fast as they can. Breathless from the exertion, they don't speak for the first five minutes, then Zoe's inquisitiveness gets the better of her and she peppers

Jake with questions about the teen ghosts and the phantom demon.

Jake does his best to answer, though he doesn't have all the information she wants, like if the phantom demon will be able to follow them home or work out where they live, though he is able to describe the exact shape of the bell-bottoms the ghosts wore and tell her that they were part of a rock band.

After Jake has answered her questions, Zoe is both scared and a little excited by the turn of events, though mainly scared. 'You know, if I hadn't seen the phantom demon with my own eyes, I'm not sure I would have believed a single word you just said.'

Jake agrees with his bestie. 'I wouldn't have either.'

Ten minutes of riding later, they zip into their quiet, leafy street, still paranoid about the phantom demon making an appearance. Before they peel off to their respective houses, they agree to message each other if anything weird happens during the night. Then they organise to meet at eight sharp the next morning, ready to hunt for JF Waronika, whose name, Zoe thinks, sounds like a puzzle waiting to be solved.

Jake is still uneasy when he arrives home. What if the phantom demon figures out where he lives and comes for him in the dead of night? And if it does, how will it happen? Will it slip in through the gap under the front door then rise above him from the shadows at the foot of his bed? Not knowing is worse than any nightmare his mind can conjure.

He keeps glancing out the window, scanning the street, expecting to see a dark shape lurking among the trees. Then it hits him. Once the sun sets and it's dark outside, he won't see it coming. And that makes it even worse.

At dinner, Jake momentarily forgets about the phantom demon when he has to explain to the PUs about the week of detention The Fossil gave him. They had received an email from the old codger just before Jake arrived home. The PUs don't go off on him as badly as he was expecting, probably because school finishes in a week's time and his report this semester was pretty good, though they do remind him to keep his smart-alec comments to himself.

Jake doesn't mention anything about the ghostly business, because involving the PUs only ever makes stuff more complicated and why would they believe it anyway? Jake hardly believes it himself.

The PUs then head to the Johnsons' place across the street for their regular Friday night drinks and nibbles, which is the one moment of weekly excitement in their extremely mid and sad social lives. In keeping with their directive to keep his smart-alec comments to himself, Jake does not mention this to them.

It's always a relief when the PUs are out of the house – though tonight, being alone isn't ideal. Every creak and murmur sends a jolt of fear through Jake as he imagines the phantom demon has arrived. So, to take his mind off that, at least a little, he decides he must shred on his guitar.

His mum once told him it takes ten thousand hours of practice to become *really* good at something. He did the math and worked out that if he practises the guitar three hours a day, every day, he should be able to get his ten thou' done in nine-and-a-bit years, which works out nicely considering he will have just turned twenty-one and the band he plans to start very soon will, by then, be ready to take on the world.

He's been keeping track of his hours in the notes app of his phone. So far, he has two hundred and twenty-four under his belt. Not bad, but he has a long, long way to go. He just has to spend every spare moment he can practising.

He decides that tonight will be his first three-hour practice sesh. He grabs his council clean-up acoustic (because Rockenstein is not yet ready to rock) then sits to start – and feels something jab into his thigh. He reaches into his pocket and pulls out the gold pick that he used to play Ricky's Telecaster earlier. He must have slipped it in there when the ghosts turned up. If he can't practise with that epic guitar, he can at least use the pick that came with it.

He spends the first hour and a half using it to rehearse basic chords and transitions, then strumming patterns, then, the hardest part, finger placement. He's trying to create calluses on his fingertips so it doesn't hurt so much when he presses down on the strings. He's also trying to play in a way that makes him look super cool, or at least cool, though he's not sure if he's pulling it off.

After that, Jake pulls out JF's notebook to see how good this kid was at songwriting. The band's set list is written on one of the pages and says their opening song was 'Hot City Rock'. Jake is happy to report that the song is there and none of the lyrics are faded or missing.

And yes, JF is talented.

The song's music is easy to read and fun to play and rips along. Jake practises it, thinking that if he gets the chance to perform rhythm guitar with the band tomorrow night, at least he'll know what's up.

Jake also practises the second song on the set list, 'Never Too Late', and then the last song, 'One and Only'. He's so in the zone that by the end of the three hours, he has forgotten about the phantom demon.

But the moment his head hits the pillow and the lights go out, his thoughts snap back to that chilling apparition. Again, every squeak and rumble from outside the house sends a spasm of terror through him. Sleep is impossible. He almost messages Zoe, then thinks better of it and decides he won't contact her unless the thing actually shows up.

So, Jake lies in his bed, eyes wide open, heart pounding, mind spinning with thoughts of dread. Shadows dance on the ceiling and with every rustling leaf from the tree outside his window, he's convinced the wraith is about to strike.

Then he hears it.

A sound from his closet.

He bolts upright in bed, the corners of his room suddenly darker than before. His breath catches, every nerve screaming at him to run. Then the sound comes again, louder this time, a rumble followed by a thud.

His stomach twists.

The phantom demon is in his closet.

But how did it get in there?

The air vent.

It must have entered through the closet's air vent. There's one in the bottom corner, right behind where he keeps his shoes.

Jake's body locks up, paralysed by the very thought of it. Then something deeper stirs, a defiance born from years of refusing to be afraid of what's in his closet. He's never been that guy and he's not going to start now.

He must go on the attack.

His eyes flick to his sports bag that lies on the floor beside his desk. It's long and wide and when empty, the perfect size to confine something that should not exist in this world.

He quietly swings his legs over the edge of his bed. His movements are measured and deliberate as he moves to the sports bag, kneels beside it, quietly unzips it, then unpacks his basketball gear onto the floor.

The empty bag clutched in his right hand, Jake creeps towards the closet. His breath comes in shallow gasps as his trembling left hand reaches for the metal doorknob. It feels cold against his palm as he takes a final breath, holds it as if his life depends on it, then with a burst of courage yanks the door open –

A mass of blackness erupts from inside, glowing eyes burning like embers as it surges towards him, a living shadow that screams malice, its form distorting and writhing as if defying gravity.

Jake barely has time to react as he swings the open bag towards it with all his strength –

CHAPTER SIX

THE bag misses its target and the dark mass scampers away with a startled yowl. Jake stumbles back, heart hammering, as he watches his family's black tabby cat, who for some reason was named Goldie by his Parental Units, dart across the room.

'Bad cat!' Jake says, half-laughing, as relief washes over him. 'No biscuits for you today, buddy!'

After Jake lets the cat out of his room, he messages Zoe and tells her what happened, which she finds pretty funny, then he goes back to bed. But he doesn't sleep well. Or at all. Every noise sets his nerves on edge until his phone's alarm goes off at the crack of dawn. Even though he's exhausted, he's thrilled to get up and get moving. Somehow, he's not as creeped out by the idea of a phantom demon attack in daylight.

He gets dressed, messages the PUs a quick note saying he'll be at the school library all day and at the Holiday Concert all night, then heads out. They like to know where he is but need nothing more. They are the *opposite* of helicopter parents and champion the whole 'free-range' approach to raising independent kids, which means they mostly let him do what he likes as long as he doesn't get into too much trouble. And their enthusiasm for his extracurricular school activities rarely rises above zero, so that makes days like today blissfully hassle-free. Thankfully, Zoe's parents are pretty cruisy too.

At exactly eight sharp, he arrives at Zoe's house, where she's already waiting on the street. Bleary-eyed and running on fumes, Jake mutters, 'I don't think I slept for a minute.'

'Oh no, it sounds like you're – *cat*-atonic.' Zoe grins.

Jake stares at her, unamused.

'What's the matter? *Cat* got your tongue?' She can't help but chuckle at that one.

Jake holds his stare, stone-faced.

'Sorry! I'll cut it out right *meow*.'

Jake gives in and smiles. 'That joke was a – *cat*-astrophe.'

They both laugh at this and a moment later they're on their bikes, pedalling towards school with the morning breeze at their backs.

The plan is clear: Scour the library for any mention of young Master JF, starting with the old school yearbooks, which are called *The Educator*.

As they get closer to the campus, the thought of facing the phantom demon again looms heavy in Jake's mind, each turn of the pedal tightening the knot in his chest. It's enough for him to glance at Zoe. 'Are you a little . . .' He trails off, not wanting to say 'freaked out'.

Zoe nods, her face uncharacteristically serious. 'More than a little.'

Jake lets out a nervous laugh. 'Good to know I'm not alone.'

Zoe shoots him a grin. 'Me too.'

Jake and Zoe see no sign of the phantom demon as they park their bikes and make their way towards the huge, three-storey library. It's pretty early for a Saturday, so it's not a surprise it's empty of students. Jake can't see the librarian anywhere. He must have nipped down to the staffroom to grab coffee from the espresso machine.

Jake and Zoe climb the wooden stairs to the second floor, where *The Educator* archive is located. The level looks out through a gigantic, panoramic window onto the sprawling sports field beyond, where two soccer teams are warming up.

The duo quickly find the rack where *The Educators* are kept and search for any from the early 1970s where, they imagine, a young JF Waronika might feature. Zoe finds the 1971 edition, and then the one from '72. She passes Jake the former and they both take a seat on the sofa. Unfortunately, there's no index to highlight if a specific student is mentioned in the yearbook, so they must read every musty, mind-numbingly dull page.

Jake opens his yearbook to a black-and-white picture of the main sports field. The photo seems to have been taken from pretty much where he and Zoe sit right now, but fifty years ago. He looks up from the photo and studies the field. Nothing much has changed, except for the scoreboard –

Hold on.

Both soccer teams are huddled around something at the edge of the field.

What are they staring at?

As if on cue, they part and give Jake a look at it. Instantly, his skin breaks out in a cold sweat. He reaches over and taps Zoe's shoulder. She glances up from her yearbook, then notices Jake's shaken expression and mouths one word: *What?*

Jake points a finger out the window and whispers: 'That.'

Zoe follows his finger towards the field below where, for all to see, the drums and cymbals that made up the Drum Hulk are scattered across the grass.

'Jeepers.' Zoe takes a moment to process what she's seeing then whispers: 'Why'd it stop there?'

Jake whispers a reply: 'The ghosts said the longer the phantom demon is in the world of the living, the more powerful it becomes. I don't think it was powerful enough to follow us all the way home last night, so that's where it ended up.'

'Where is it now?'

Jake shrugs. 'Don't know, but it must have moved on to something else.' He scans the area, then points again. 'Like that!' This time his finger is aimed at a see-through mesh bag that contains one, two, three, four, five soccer balls.

One by one, the balls squeeze through the top of the bag then start to roll across the field – straight towards the building where Jake and Zoe are located. They watch the balls quickly move to the edge of the field, then up a grassy incline, then up a short series of steps and then onto the walkway below the library building.

Jake is on guard as he and Zoe lose sight of the soccer balls. 'We should go.'

Zoe nods. 'Okay, but I found something.' She points to a page in the 1972 edition of *The Educator*. 'It's in the creative writing section. It's about a kid's first day at school. And it's signed JF Waronika.'

'Excellent, but how does it help us?'

'It names the street he lives on.'

Jake's eyes light up. 'Oh my god, Zozz for the win. You legend. Take a pic.'

Zoe whips out her phone and takes a photo of the short story, then they swiftly move down the wooden stairs, each step creaking under their weight.

The vast library stretches below them, its towcring shclvcs casting dccp, ominous shadows in the pale morning light. No other students have made an appearance yet and the librarian is still missing in action, so the place is eerily silent.

At the bottom of the stairs, Jake stops abruptly, his face pale as he points towards the far side of the room and whispers: 'They're already here.'

Zoe's breath hitches in her throat as a soccer ball rolls between the shelves with creepy precision. There's something profoundly off about it, its movements deliberate and calculating. It halts suddenly, then rotates as though searching the room for prey.

'It's hunting us,' Zoe whispers, finding the words difficult to believe.

Jake's jaw tightens. He nods, then turns to look for an escape route – and finds one. 'This way.' They dart behind a bookshelf so it can't see them, then move quickly and quietly along an aisle towards the glass doors at the library's entrance –

Another soccer ball trundles into view at the end of the aisle. Jake and Zoe stop, then retreat into the shadows, holding their breath. The ball pauses and pivots, scanning for them, its black-and-white leather panels warped and twisted, its seams bulging as if something alive and malevolent is trapped within.

It searches for another moment, then rolls on –

As Jake exhales, his hip touches the shelf behind him. Not very hard but hard enough to make it rattle.

The ball swivels to the sound and with a sudden jolt launches itself at him. Jake ducks out of the way and it smashes into the shelf behind him with such force that it topples over, sending a cascade of books crashing to the floor.

The duo are now exposed. Zoe yells, 'Run!' and they sprint for the glass doors as three more soccer balls hurtle towards them like they've been shot out of a cannon.

Boom! One slams into Jake's thigh, sending a sharp pain shooting down his leg. He stumbles but keeps running as Zoe boots the ball away.

Bam! Another smashes into his shoulder and spins him around. 'Son of a –' He grits it out and doesn't stop moving. Again, Zoe dispatches the ball to the other side of the library with a swift kick.

Wham! A third ball strikes Jake in the chest and knocks the wind out of him. He staggers but refuses to stop, pure adrenaline propelling him forward. With a sharp jab of her foot, Zoe sends the ball flying.

They both turn to the glass doors that loom in front of them. They're about to get out of here –

Then the fifth ball rolls into view – right in front of those glass doors.

In all the excitement, Jake and Zoe forgot about the fifth ball.

But it didn't forget about them.

It rockets towards the duo like an Mbappé shot at goal in the dying moments of a World Cup final. Before Jake can devise a plan, Zoe decides to give this ball a red card. She rushes forward and swings her leg to kick it –

The soccer ball bounces *over* her foot and flies straight at Jake's face. He sees it coming and manages to duck his head like he's going to head it away – but then the ball's leather panels split at the seams to create a gruesome, gaping mouth that wraps around his head like it's a Chupa Chup.

Fwup! Everything in Jake's world instantly turns black and his nose is filled with that putrid smell.

But that's not the worst thing.

No, the worst thing is that he *can't breathe*.

CHAPTER SEVEN

JAKE tries to yank the ball off his head.

It does not work.

The little sucker is really stuck on there. It's like trying to get out of a tight, damp wetsuit – while the wetsuit is trying to *kill you*.

'Help!' he calls to Zoe, but the word is just a muffled grunt. Anyway, she doesn't have to be asked. He can feel her grab and pull at the soccer ball. And he can feel it move on his head – just not enough.

So, this is how it ends?

Smothered by a soccer ball because he wanted to help a teen ghost rock group escape Limbo and move on to the afterlife.

He's not sure anyone could have predicted that.

Jake suddenly feels light-headed, but he pushes it away, tries to focus on a way out of this.

He just can't think of one.

Then he can.

The *pick*!

He remembers the gold guitar pick from the Telecaster's case. After rehearsing with it last night, he tucked it into his wallet for safekeeping.

Jake dives a hand into the right side pocket of his pants to grab the wallet.

Not there.

He tries the left side pocket.

No.

Where the hell is it?

He feels dizzy now.

Push it away.

It's in your back pocket, buddy.

Jake plunges a hand into the back pocket – and pulls out his wallet. He moves to quickly open it but fumbles and drops it.

Oh no!

He bends to find it on the floor – then a hand places it in his.

Zozz to the rescue!

This time Jake takes his time to carefully open the wallet so he doesn't drop it. He pulls out the metal pick, grabs it by the wide end and drives its sharp point into the soccer ball where it covers his mouth.

Thump.

The metal cuts into the leather but doesn't puncture it. So, he tries again.

Thump.

It doesn't puncture it.

He feels really dizzy now.

Push it away.

For the third time he drives the metal guitar pick into the soccer ball that is trying to suffocate him.

Thump!

The leather is punctured. It's not a very big hole but it's big enough and he pulls in a lung full of lovely, fresh air.

It feels so, so good.

Then he sticks two fingers into the small hole and yanks it open with all his might. The leather tears apart more easily than he thought it would and he wrenches the soccer ball off his head and flings it across the hallway.

It slams into the wall and immediately tries to roll its deflated self back towards Jake –

Whump. Zoe stamps her foot down and traps it, then turns to Jake, deeply concerned. 'You okay?'

Jake nods as he drags in a couple of big breaths. Zoe points at the deflated soccer ball beneath her foot. 'What do we do with this?'

Before Jake can answer, the soccer ball erupts with a deafening crack and spews forth the phantom demon in a swirling, inky mass. Zoe jumps back as the shadowy figure shoots towards the ceiling, its form stretching and writhing unnaturally. As it spirals higher, two glowing eyes emerge from within the dark smoke, burning embers of crimson that pierce through the shadows with a hateful, predatory glare.

They lock onto Jake and Zoe, seething with an unspoken promise of doom.

Zoe recoils, her face twisting into a grimace. 'It doesn't get any less spooky the second time you see it.'

With a violent surge, the phantom demon blasts through the gap in the skylight, its dark tendrils trailing behind it before it vanishes into the blue sky beyond, leaving behind an oppressive silence.

Zoe turns to Jake, clearly freaked out. 'Where did it go?'

Jake shakes his head grimly. 'Don't know, but I do know it's more powerful than it was yesterday.'

*

We used to move a lot and I went to lots of schools. Then I found out I got into this school and I was so happy. The teachers are nice and so are the boys and the girls. There will be no more moving. I'm going to live at 17 Alison Place for a long, long time.

Jack F Waronika, Class 4B

Sitting on their bikes, Jake and Zoe study JF's creative writing entry in *The Educator*, the image glowing on Zoe's phone. After a quick Google search, Jake discovers there's only one Alison Place within two hundred and fifty kilometres, and it's only ten minutes away on their bikes. The discovery feels like a stroke of luck, maybe even fate.

'What if he still lives there?' Jake wonders aloud, excitement flickering in his voice.

Zoe nods but her expression is cautious. 'I mean, what are the chances, right? Could it be that easy?'

Without hesitation, they set off towards JF Waronika's childhood home. The ride is quiet, the only sounds the rhythmic crunch of their tyres on the road and the rustle of the breeze through the trees overhead.

Jake notices Zoe's silence. It's not like her to be so subdued. Like, ever. She normally has a dad joke or a funny comment ready to go. Their last encounter with the phantom demon must have really spooked her.

After a moment, Jake breaks the ice. 'Look, it's totally fine if you don't want to keep doing this. Seriously.'

Zoe shoots him a sharp look, like he's pulled that thought straight out of her head. 'Why would you say that?'

'Because, up until now, it's only been after me. But if you keep going, it might come for you. The ghosts said that could happen.'

Fear ripples across Zoe's face, but she immediately shakes it off. 'I don't want that, obviously, but I'm not backing out. I want to solve this thing, even if it takes me a while to get my head around it.'

'Fair enough,' Jake says with a smile. He's very glad she doesn't want to quit.

They ride on for a moment, then Zoe turns to Jake. 'Did you know that I can see into the future?'

Jake grins. Excellent. A bad joke from Zoe means she's feeling better. He plays along. 'Really? Since when?'

'Next Tuesday.'

They laugh at that and swerve down the steep, tree-shrouded Livingston Avenue. This suburb feels unsettlingly remote, despite being close to the highway and train station. There's no traffic, no people, just the eerie, oppressive roar of crickets. The surrounding bushland seems to watch them, its stillness unnerving.

Now that he knows the phantom demon has gained power, Jake can't shake the feeling that it's lurking out there, stalking them. His chest tightens with a creeping sense of dread, his instincts screaming danger. He keeps his eyes sharp, scanning the trees and shadows around him, but he doesn't say anything to Zoe. No point in freaking her out; at least, not until he's sure there's something to be freaked out about.

They turn into Alison Place and find number 17 situated at the end of a cul-de-sac. It's a simple house built yonks ago that could do with a little TLJ (Tender Loving Jake) to tidy it up. Unfortunately, it's empty, and looks like it's been that way for years. So, Jake and Zoe's hope that this could all be solved with one quick conversation with the actual guy, who would remember the exact lyrics he wrote fifty years ago and want to play in the concert tonight, goes out the window.

As they ride away, Jake can't help but be disappointed. He has no idea how he's going to find JF –

'Get off my lawn!' The shrill voice wrenches Jake out of his thoughts as a long, thin wooden stick flashes into his field of view and lodges between the large spokes of his BMX bike's front wheel.

Before he can say 'What the –' the stick brings Jake's front wheel to a dead stop, which, in turn, brings the bike to a dead stop. Unfortunately, it doesn't bring *Jake* to a dead stop. Instead, he flies over the handlebars, sails awkwardly through the air then face plants on what he thinks might be the softest and most luxurious grass he's ever touched.

'Jake!' Zoe skids her bike to a halt and looks down at her mate. 'You okay?'

Jake nods as he spits out a mouthful of lawn. 'I'm all right.'

They turn to an old man who stands nearby, wears a faded dressing gown and laughs wildly. His messy white hair and beard jut out like he's been struck by lightning, while his bony hands clutch a rusted rake, held backward, the handle of which was just used to stop Jake's bike. 'Wow. You really ate it, boy! Got room for dessert?'

The old man's eyes glint with cruel delight as he laughs again, this time revealing teeth so yellow they'd make a banana jealous. Then his laughter abruptly cuts off and he snaps: 'Now get off my lawn!'

'We're not on your lawn!' Jake says as he sits up and picks the grass out of his teeth.

'You're on it right now!'

'What are you talking about?' Jake finds his feet and brushes the grass off his clothes. 'No, I'm not.'

Zoe chimes in. 'Yeah, he's on the nature strip.'

'It's my lawn!' This old bloke is very insistent, and very old, if that wasn't already clear. 'Mine.'

Zoe has had enough of this guy. 'Okay, grandpa, pipe down. It's a public footpath.'

A spark flickers behind the old man's eyes and he grins. 'Hold on! I know you! You're from that school. The one a couple of stations up the train line. I'm going to report the both of you. What's that place called again? Oh geez.' Old Mate racks his brain for the answer to his own question and Jake almost feels bad for him. 'That kid, who lived across the street. He used to go there.'

Jake and Zoe look at each other, stunned, then Jake asks: 'You don't mean JF, do you? JF Waronika?'

'Of course I do! Who else would I be talking about?'

Jake can't believe his ears but plays along. 'Exactly, who else.'

Then the old man turns to them, confused. 'Hold on, how would you know him?'

'Well, we're actually looking for him right now. That's why we're here.'

'He used to ride on my nature strip too.' The old man smiles, as if fondly remembering a great time from years ago. 'I got him good a couple of times.'

Zoe just can't with this guy, but Jake keeps it nice. 'So, is there any chance you might know where he lives now?'

'Why? Do you want to ride on his nature strip too?'

Jake ignores that and stays pleasant. 'Oh no, we'd just like to visit him.'

'Like I asked before: why?'

'Well, he went to our school and we had questions about what it was like back in the day.' Zoe tries to sell it by pointing a thumb over her shoulder like that's where the past lives.

Horrible Santa squints at her. 'I have no idea where he is. All I can remember is that his father had a heart attack and died. Then his mother got married quick smart and took her new husband's name. So did the kid. He wasn't called Waronika anymore.'

'Do you remember what his new name was?' Jake hopes to hell he knows.

Old fella makes a big show of trying to remember, but Jake can see he hasn't got the foggiest idea, so when he shakes his head, it's no big surprise.

Zoe chimes in. 'Do you think anyone else in the street might remember –'

Before she can finish the question, the old man shakes his head again. 'Everyone has moved away or carked it.'

As this information washes over Jake, he knows it's the worst-case scenario. Their only lead has led to nothing. He glances at Zoe and sees the same frustration mirrored in her face.

'We should get moving,' she says quietly, her voice hollow.

Jake nods, unable to muster a verbal response. They climb onto their bikes in silence and pedal away, the weight of failure bearing down on them.

'Hey! Where are you going?!' the old codger yells after them, his voice sharp and cutting. 'I'm not done with you yet! Do you hear me? I'm not done!'

But Jake is. He hears Awful Grandad's words but they are drowned out by a more pressing thought: they don't even know JF's *name*. And if they don't know his name, how in the world are they supposed to find him?

CHAPTER EIGHT

JAKE and Zoe pedal in silence.

The disappointment hangs heavy between them.

Jake reluctantly accepts that their plan to find JF is dead in the water. They have two-thirds of the song but no way to track down the man who knows the final piece. Jake will have to summon the ghost band back to the attic at Nocturne House and tell them he failed.

Actually, it's worse than disappointing.

It's embarrassing.

The road stretches on. There are no cars, no people, just the thrum of their bikes' tyres on asphalt and that oppressive sound of crickets.

Jake tries his best to ignore it until another pressure makes itself known.

'I need a bathroom break.' Jake says it as he slows his bike.

Zoe brakes too. 'Knock yourself out.'

'I'll be quick.' Jake points at an empty, overgrown lot beside a rambling old house and pedals towards it.

Zoe nods. 'That's the best thing about the great outdoors for guys. It's one big toilet.'

Jake laughs and it momentarily drags him out of his funk. They pull up beside the old house, which has seen better days, its knee-high grass wild and chaotic, while the structure itself is hunched and sad.

Jake drops his bike in the long grass and moves to the vacant lot. 'Won't be a sec.'

'Make it snappy.' Zoe keeps her eyes peeled as she climbs off her bike and takes a swig from her water bottle.

Jake crunches through overgrown foliage, the sun beating down on his shoulders as the shrill racket of insects rises around him. He pushes deeper into the lot, finds a spot behind a gnarled old tree where he's almost sure he can't be seen from the road, then gets down to business.

A moment later he finishes, walks back through that long grass and arrives at the bikes.

Zoe isn't there.

He looks around but can't see any sign of her.

What the?

Fear rising in his chest, he calls out. 'Zozz?'

'Shhh! Keep your voice down!' comes her whispered response.

'Where are you?'

'Shhh! Get down!'

Then he sees her, crouched in the long grass to the left, her face pale. She motions him over, hand trembling. He kneels beside her and keeps his voice low: 'What's going on?'

Zoe points into the garden of the neighbouring house. Jake follows her finger and his stomach drops.

The phantom demon floats behind a thicket, its twisted form pulsating with dark energy. It moves with unnatural grace as it searches – no, hunts – for them.

'It's so much bigger than before,' Zoe whispers.

Jake tries to process that it has almost *doubled* in size since they last saw it. 'It's bigger than my *dad*.'

He says it too loudly.

The phantom demon abruptly turns and glides towards them, its swirling ribbons of black smoke and shadow curling through the air like death adders, ready to strike.

'I told you to keep your voice down,' reprimands Zoe in a low whisper.

As the supernatural creature sweeps across the low fence that separates the gardens, the duo flatten themselves to the ground, the rough grass stabbing at their skin. Still, they don't move, don't twitch, don't even breathe.

Then the stench hits them, choking and thick, making their eyes water and stomachs churn.

The phantom demon slows, its jagged tendrils curling downward, brushing the grass inches above their heads –

Wham! A car door slams in the distance.

The phantom demon's shadowy form twists unnaturally as it changes direction and glides towards the sound.

A long moment passes.

Then another.

Then Jake cautiously pokes his head up above the grass and scans the area.

He can see no sign of the dark apparition. 'We need to get out of here,' he whispers, his voice urgent.

Zoe nods. Together, they stay low in the long grass, their movements steady and deliberate until they reach their bikes and climb on.

Then Jake's phone rings.

Now, most people have their ringtone set to silent, but not Jake. He likes it loud and proud. And that's because he has the opening guitar riff of his favourite new *old song* as his ringtone.

It's from 'What I Like About You' by a 1970s band called The Romantics. He discovered it on YouTube a month ago when he was looking for rock songs with punchy, melodic guitar riffs that he could teach himself.

'Turn it off!' Zoe hisses, panic rising in her voice.

Jake sees it's another in a long line of spam calls and declines it, but the damage has been done.

The shrubs beside the old house thrash violently then the phantom demon rises above them, its shadow stretching over the lot like a living nightmare.

Jake stares at it with icy dread. 'We gotta move!'

He and Zoe kick their bikes into motion as the phantom demon sweeps down and crashes into the overgrown grass right behind them, sending a shockwave through the garden.

A moment passes.

Then another.

Zoe glances over her shoulder, then has to quickly look again to make sure her eyes aren't playing tricks on her. 'What the?!'

Jake hears her and looks back – then recoils as a dozen old garden gnomes burst out of the long grass.

Yes, the lawn ornaments have sprung to life, their once-innocent faces twisted into bloodthirsty sneers and malevolent scowls as they lunge forward with sinister intent.

Legs pumping like pistons, Jake and Zoe pedal furiously along the road. They pull away but the gnomes are relentless as their tiny feet clatter and clank on the bitumen in disturbing syncopation.

Then the road gets steeper.

Jake and Zoe slow down.

'We gotta go faster!' yells Jake.

'This *is* faster!' replies Zoe, her voice strained with exertion.

The steep slope turns every push of their pedals into a gruelling battle against gravity.

Jake chances a look back.

The gnomes are closer.

Much closer.

One, dressed like a sinister Santa Claus, leaps high and lands on Jake's back. Its rough ceramic hands claw at his helmet as it shrieks in a high-pitched battle cry.

'Ahhh!' Jake franticly swipes at it with a hand but the gnome clings on with an unnaturally strong grip.

'Get off, you little –' Jake swings a fist and clocks the pint-sized Santa in the face. The gnome drops to the ground and shatters with a sharp, satisfying crack.

But there's no time to celebrate.

Another gnome, painted in the twisted blue of a demonic Smurf, launches itself at Zoe with a bloodthirsty screech. She dodges it and the little sucker thumps into her front tyre with a bone-jarring thud. The force catapults it high into the air, spinning wildly before it slams into a parked car and explodes in a shower of jagged shards.

The top of the hill looms before Jake and Zoe, though it still feels impossibly far away. They grit their teeth and lean into the climb. Sweat drips and muscles burn as they ride with everything they've got, determined to reach the summit.

Meanwhile, the gnomes keep on coming. One, resembling a deranged hobbit, lunges at Jake. It latches onto his thigh with feral determination and sinks its jagged teeth into his jeans.

'Ahhh!' The pain is terrible. 'Get off, you little horror show!' Jake tries to swat it away but the evil hobbit doesn't budge. Then it goes in for another bite –

Boom! With deadly precision, Zoe kicks the gnome off Jake's leg. It spirals through the air and smashes on the road with a satisfying crunch.

Jake and Zoe finally reach the crest of the hill.

Before them lies a steep, twisting, downhill run. They grip their handlebars and launch down the incline. The pitter-patter of tiny ceramic feet recedes behind them as the ground blurs beneath their tyres.

Jake risks another glance behind him. The gnomes have fallen back, their short legs no match for the bikes' speed. Relief floods through him –

Then he spots it.

There is one gnome following them.

But it isn't running.

It's riding.

And it's catching them.

The overachiever is dressed in green like a fun-size Robin Hood and charges after them atop a galloping dachshund, the ceramic dog's teeth bared in a wild, undomesticated snarl. The gnome raises a tiny bow and, with wicked precision, lets an arrow fly.

Ping! The arrow ricochets off Jake's rear wheel.

'What the?!' Jake can't believe his eyes. 'One of them is *shooting* at us!'

The overachiever reloads, its weathered face twisted into a sinister grin, and fires again.

Thud! The arrow slams into Zoe's bottle and pierces it clean through. A spout of water streams out and splatters her leg.

The overachiever throws its head back and cackles a shrill, maniacal laugh that carries on the wind. It then reloads with chilling efficiency, draws another arrow – and takes aim with unnerving focus at Jake's head . . .

CHAPTER NINE

CRUNCH.

The ancient, beaten-up ute that backs out of the driveway never sees the gnomes because it doesn't have a reversing camera. It drives out at just the right moment and crushes them under its rear wheels, then does the same thing again with its front wheels.

The driver, a young man with the Bushwick Mullet that is the popular haircut of the moment (short and tight on the side, long and flowing at the back, bowl cut of regret at the front) doesn't seem to notice and probably thinks the cracking sounds beneath his tyres are just the large chunks of bark that fall from the towering gum trees that line this street.

None the wiser, Bushwick Mullet casually pulls onto the road and drives past the stunned and thankful Jake and Zoe.

'Grab hold! We need to get as far away from the phantom demon as fast as possible,' Jake yells as he grasps the ute's tailgate.

Zoe doesn't hesitate. She grabs hold too and they're whisked away from the gnomes' flattened remains. They look back just in time to see the fragments begin to tremble. Then, with a violent blast, the phantom demon erupts from the shards. Its malevolent shadow coils upward like a serpent before vanishing into the canopy of trees above.

'How long will it take to find us?' Zoe asks, her voice grave.

Jake turns to his friend. 'I don't know, but when we summon the band, it'll know where we are.'

Zoe's lips press into a thin line as she unhappily takes this in.

For nearly five minutes, they cling to the ute as it rumbles along the road, the world rushing past in a blur. Then Bushwick Mullet catches sight of them in his rearview mirror. Furious, he leans out the window and barks at them: 'Hey! You two! Rack off! Before you get yourselves killed!'

Jake and Zoe share a sheepish grin then release their grip on the ute and dart down a side street. They ride hard, urgency powering every turn of their pedals as they race to school and a date with the ghost band. Jake desperately hopes they can remember something that might help them locate JF.

They park their bikes and, with eyes scanning for any sign of the phantom demon, hurry past the snarling gargoyle crouched above the entrance to Nocturne House before ascending to the shadowy attic.

Jake is thrilled to open the guitar case and see the Telecaster again. It's more gorgeous than he remembered, even with its flame-grilled back. He plugs it in, then reaches into his back pocket and pulls out the guitar pick that saved his life.

Zoe watches, excited but anxious. 'So, I finally get to meet the ghosts.'

Jake nods. Zoe nods too then her anxiousness overwhelms her excitement. Jake sees it. 'You all right?'

She does her best to keep it together. 'Bit nervous. The last time I met a spectral entity from the netherworld it tried to shoot me with a bow and arrow.'

'Well, this lot are good people,' responds Jake. 'They're *dead* people but they're *good* people.'

She forces a brave smile. 'I bet they are.'

'Okay. You ready?'

Zoe takes a breath, then: 'Let it rock, baby.'

'And remember, as soon as I do this, the phantom demon is going to know where we are.'

Zoe nods as Jake takes the neck of the guitar in hand, lets his fingers find the strings, raises the pick high – then swings it down and perfectly strums the chord of E minor 9.

The sound blasts from the amp and reverberates across the attic. In a flash, three ripples appear, growing and twisting into a spinning tunnel. Light blasts from its depths and floods the room with that eerie, golden glow as the air whips into a roaring cyclone that sends papers flying in a chaotic swirl.

Zoe's eyes widen in amazement as she watches the three glowing, translucent figures sweep out of the tunnel then materialise into the teenage ghost band known as Ricky & the Blue Jeans.

'Wow. You look way better than I thought. I was expecting full-on zombie mode with flesh falling off and eyeballs missing.' She winces. 'Okay, that came out wrong. What I meant was, you're dead and dead people usually look dead. But you look alive even though you're dead.' She winces again. 'Whatever. I'm not apologising. I think I'm handling my first paranormal conversation really well.'

Ricky stares at her, perplexed. 'Who are you?'

Jake answers. 'She's my friend. Zoe.'

Ricky is still perplexed. 'And who are you?' He has no idea who Jake is. In fact, none of the band do.

Now Zoe is perplexed. 'What's happening?'

Jake turns to her and whispers, 'The longer you spend in Limbo the more your memory starts to fade.' He looks back to the band. 'It's me. Jake. I'm helping you leave Limbo. Remember, we met yesterday.'

Timbo studies Jake. 'Really?'

'Yes, really. You're going to perform at the school concert in, like,' Jake looks at his phone, 'an hour.'

As Jake says it, he can see the band slowly start to recall. JoBeth is the first to get there. 'Oh! Jake.' She turns to Timbo and Ricky. 'You remember Jake. He was going to look for JF.'

Ricky remembers. 'That's right.'

And then so does Timbo. 'Jake. From yesterday.'

Jake nods. 'Yes, Jake. From yesterday. And this is my friend, Zoe. She's been helping me.' Jake pulls the leather-bound notebook from his back pocket. 'Look. JF's notebook. All his songs are in here.'

Zoe eagerly raises her hand. 'That was me! I found that!'

Jake passes the notebook to Ricky, who accepts it with a gracious nod. 'Thank you.' The other ghosts crowd around him as he opens it and flips through the pages. He lands on 'One and Only'. 'Oh! That's how it goes.'

The band have a joint epiphany as they recall the song.

'I remember it now.' Timbo smiles.

And so does JoBeth. 'JF was *so good* with lyrics.'

Ricky can barely contain his excitement. 'I can't believe you found this. This is our ticket out of Limbo.'

'As long as the phantom demon doesn't turn up,' Jake adds. 'And on that note, we need to wind this up pretty fast before it works out where we are –'

Clank.

A loud sound reverberates behind Jake.

His stomach drops.

Too late.

It's already here.

He spins around, on guard, ready to fight the phantom demon where he stands –

But it's just Zoe closing the window. 'Sorry, got a bit chilly in here.'

Jake breathes a sigh of relief, then looks back at Ricky, who turns another page of the notebook and sees the print has faded. Jake grimaces: 'It's all there except for the final verse of "One and Only".'

Timbo rubs his ghost face, dismayed. 'We need the whole song.'

Jake nods. 'I know.'

'Did you find JF?'

Zoe answers that: 'We tried. His mum got remarried. He literally changed his surname and moved away.'

Jake confirms that with a nod. 'Do you have anything else that might help us find him?'

The band exchange glances then shake their heads.

Jake's shoulders sag, then he's struck by a thought and turns to the others. 'Did you guys ever perform the missing lyrics in front of anyone?'

The band shake their heads.

'And you didn't finish it on the night you . . . you know –' Jake hesitates, lowering his voice, '– carked it.'

The band members shake their heads again.

'So, no-one knows what the lyrics actually are! Which means they can be whatever we want them to be.' Jake knows he's grasping at straws but goes with it.

'But *we've* heard them,' Timbo counters.

Jake presses on. 'Yeah, but you don't *remember* them. So technically, they can be anything. Maybe we write some new ones.'

The band exchanges uncertain glances, then JoBeth speaks: 'Look, if we don't try, we're stuck in Limbo forever. But if we do try, it either works or we're still stuck in Limbo forever. So really, we've got nothing to lose.'

Ricky and Timbo know she's right and nod, then the five of them get to work. In less than three minutes, they've crafted a brand-new third verse to the song.

Ricky insists on rehearsing it but Jake is uneasy. 'Guys, the phantom demon could show up at any second.'

But Ricky is insistent. 'I know, but if we don't nail this song the plan fails anyway. And it'll only take a few minutes.'

Jake thinks they're pushing their luck but reluctantly agrees. 'Okay, but let's be quick.'

So, the band conjure their ghostly instruments. Timbo's four-drum, five-cymbal set-up, JoBeth's five-string bass guitar and Ricky's Stratocaster guitar. In a flash, everything is plugged in to amps, mic'd up and ready to rock 'n' roll.

Ricky glances over at Jake. 'Do you wanna play?'

Jake tries to be cool and not look too excited but fails miserably. 'Yes, please!'

Then Ricky turns to Zoe. 'How about you?'

Zoe shakes her head. 'I'm good, thanks.'

She's amazing on keyboards but doesn't like to perform with people watching. Jake almost says that but stops himself because he doesn't want to embarrass Zoe in front of the ghost teens.

So, the band plays.

The drums are tight, the bass delivers a solid groove, Ricky absolutely shreds on guitar and the vocal harmonies soar. For a bunch of teenagers who haven't been alive for half a century, they sure sound good. Jake is happy he practised the song last night because it makes all the difference to his confidence as he plays with them. For a short moment he almost forgets to keep an eye out for the phantom demon.

Almost.

After Zoe listens to the song for a bit, Jake is genuinely shocked to see her wander over to the old electric piano, switch it on and start to play. Maybe she doesn't feel self-conscious performing in front of ghosts like she does the living, because her improvisations and flourishes kill. The ghosts hear what she's doing and shoot each other impressed nods.

Jake receives no such impressed nods. While the ghosts and Zoe play with a loose and instinctive feel, he is tight and stiff and has to really concentrate on what he's doing just to stay with them. Jake realises it's going to take the full ten thousand hours of practice for him to be as confident at playing music as they are right now. For the first time, he has doubts about his dream of learning guitar and starting a band. Will all the time and effort be worth it if there's a chance he'll never be good enough?

ZANG!
THUMP THUMP THUMP
FANG!

When the song ends, the ghost teens don't hesitate, they immediately ask Zozz to join their band. And to Jake's utter shock, she says yes.

Yes!

He must have asked her to start a band with him a *bazillion* times, and on every single occasion it was a hard no. Then these ghosts turn up and play one song and she's all in!

Flabbergasted, Jake discreetly confronts her afterwards. 'Seriously? You said yes?'

Zoe brushes it off. 'Calm your farm. It's a one-and-done. I'm not signing a record deal. A single performance with zero commitment.'

Jake takes her point, but still, it's a little annoying.

A moment later the air starts to ripple behind the ghosts. Then the ripples quickly twist into a spinning tunnel as the golden light appears and the air begins to churn.

Jake is on edge and wonders if it will draw the phantom demon to them this time. He then glances at his phone. 'Forty-five minutes till showtime.'

Ricky nods. 'Okay, see you then.'

Jake then lifts a clenched fist. 'Umm, before you go, can we maybe fist bump? And say something cool like, "And the rest is rock 'n' roll history!"?'

Before anyone in the band can respond, they shift into their translucent forms and glide into the spinning tunnel, which then vanishes, leaving Jake standing awkwardly with his fist raised.

Puzzled, Zoe raises her fist too. 'So, what is this?'

Embarrassed, Jake drops this hand and plays it off. 'Nothing. Just trying something.'

Zoe's eyes narrow. 'Spill.'

Jake is incapable of keeping a secret from Zoe, so he spills.

Zoe listens thoughtfully as he explains his dream of saying something epic after his rock band crushes a song. Afterwards, Zoe nods, her expression unreadable. 'I see.'

'Is that cringe?' he wonders aloud.

'Totally.' Then she grins. 'And we should absolutely do it.'

Jake loves that. That's why they're besties.

Their next stop is Wentworth Hall, the massive auditorium set to host tonight's Holiday Concert. Jake packs up the Telecaster while Zoe loads the keyboard into its battered road case. They work fast, on high alert for any sign of the phantom demon.

Moments later, they haul their gear out of Nocturne House and emerge into the moonlit quadrangle. The sprawling, empty space feels far too exposed, setting their nerves on edge as they lug the equipment past the humongous Sports Centre on their left and the towering Chapel on their right and move towards the distant silhouette of Wentworth Hall.

That's where they will perform tonight. Outside its main entrance, Zoe is shocked to see there's already a long line of mums and dads and Chads and Mads who file in to watch the show. 'There are a lot of people there.'

Jake agrees. He's been so focused on other stuff that it hadn't fully registered that they are going to perform in front of a full house. He wonders if he'll have stage fright. He's never performed for a single person before, let alone the thousand or so who will fill the school's auditorium.

'Not to jinx it or anything,' Zoe says, 'but the phantom demon never showed.'

'Maybe it's not as powerful as we think,' Jake offers, finding it hard to believe but hoping it to be true nonetheless.

They keep moving as Zoe shoots Jake a sly grin. 'Hey, why did the phantom demon cross the road?'

Jake groans. 'Oh god. Why?'

'To get to the *other* side. Get it? *Other* side? Get it?'

Zoe elbows him in the ribs as Jake shakes his head, smirking. 'Yeah, I get it.'

They laugh at her terrible joke, the tension momentarily lifting – then the smell hits. That rancid, gut-churning stench slams into them like a truck and their smiles vanish in an instant.

'Oh no,' Jake mutters, his stomach clenching like a vice.

They freeze mid-step, then see it.

Above the Chapel, the phantom demon rises, a monstrous vortex of dark energy, writhing like a storm cloud given life.

And it's absolutely enormous.

CHAPTER TEN

THE phantom demon hovers in eerie silence, its glowing red eyes fixed on Jake and Zoe.

'It looks like the devil,' Zoe whispers, her voice trembling.

As if it heard her, the phantom demon launches itself across the night towards the duo.

Jake and Zoe move fast. Clutching their instruments, they sprint across the quadrangle to take cover in the Sports Centre, their feet pounding the ground as the monstrous force bears down on them.

The spectre plunges into the flagpole at the quadrangle's centre. The metal groans and bends as if alive, the school flag whipping violently in the air. Then, with a sharp, metallic crack, it snaps free of its base.

'Look out!' Zoe shoves Jake aside as the pole slams to the ground and just misses him. It sends a spray of dirt and grass into the air as the duo scramble through the Sports Centre's main entrance. Breathing hard, they dash down a wide hallway past rows and rows of lockers.

The phantom demon erupts from the twisted flagpole, flies through the entrance, slams into the lockers then spreads across their surface like a tsunami of black oil.

With an ear-splitting clang, the locker doors all burst open, snapping like metallic jaws. Jake dives under a high one and narrowly avoids its sharp edge, only for a low door to slam into his knee with brutal force.

'Ahhh!' The pain shoots up his leg like a lightning bolt. He just stays upright, grits his teeth and staggers forward. Zoe grabs his arm and they crash through a set of double doors onto the school's basketball court.

Behind them, a hard metallic shriek reverberates. They turn to see one of the lockers blast through the doors and lurch into the gym like a bizarre, robotic Tyrannosaur.

Jake and Zoe sprint behind the towering wooden bleachers and the rogue locker follows. It moves with a twisted, jerky movement and yet is impossibly fast.

Jake and Zoe take cover in the shadows beneath the bleachers. They don't speak or breathe, they just listen as the locker clanks towards them.

It's a predator on the hunt.

It rattles past the duo without seeing them. They wait until they can no longer hear the noise then step out of the shadows and move off in the opposite direction –

The locker is right in front of them.

Its door swings open with a deafening roar, revealing a churning, unnatural darkness inside. Jake stares into the abyss, unable to look away. It's both mesmerising and horrifying, a void of infinite depth, radiating an eerie, otherworldly beauty.

And yet, beneath its hypnotic allure lies the chilling promise of an end to all things, a consuming finality that tugs at the edges of his reality.

Jake and Zoe turn to run but the locker hurtles forward. Its door snaps shut around Jake's left leg and he cries out, the force yanking him off his feet. The guitar case crashes to the floor as the void within *drags him in*.

'Jake!' Zoe's voice cracks with terror as she drops the keyboard case, grabs his arm, plants her feet and pulls with all her might. It's a desperate tug-of-war as the locker groans and tightens its grip on her friend.

Jake winces as the locker relentlessly yanks him inside. Jake and Zoe lock eyes and instinctively know they'll never see each other again if he's pulled in completely.

Jake's hand slips through Zoe's fingers, the darkness claiming more and more of him.

Zoe summons every ounce of her strength and wrenches on Jake's arm – and he slides out. They collapse to the floor as the locker door slams shut with a deafening clang.

'Thanks,' gasps Jake, his voice shaky.

'No worries,' Zoe replies as she helps him to his feet.

The locker groans ominously then surges towards them again. Without hesitation, Jake springs forward and drives his foot into its door.

The impact echoes through the gym as the locker lets out an unholy screech, then tips over and crashes to the floor with a thunderous bang.

'Time to go.' Jake doesn't need to say it twice. Hearts pounding, they grab their instruments and sprint for the exit.

The duo burst outside and run down a long walkway to Wentworth Hall's stage door. Jake tugs it open and they race inside, then shut it behind them and peer through the door's small window.

Jake blinks away his fear and prepares for what comes next.

But nothing comes next.

The phantom demon doesn't appear.

Zoe frowns. 'Where is it?'

Jake shakes his head. He has no idea.

They continue to stare out the window – but it doesn't show.

Zoe shifts uncomfortably. 'So what, we just wait for it to turn up?'

Jake nods, but he's unsure.

Zoe exhales. 'I don't love that.'

'Neither do I.'

Jake and Zoe unhappily turn to see a bunch of students and teachers milling around in the large green room as they prepare for their performances, totally unaware of the duo's recent battle with the evil apparition.

Jake can see The Fossil fossilising about with a headset on because he's the stage manager for tonight's show. Ms Berman, the other music teacher, who's not very old, checks them in on her iPad. Jake tells her the rest of the band will be along shortly then asks if there's a place where they can rehearse. She points to room 3B.

Once Jake and Zoe are inside, they stay vigilant for any sign of the phantom demon. They hold off summoning the ghosts, in case it calls the dark entity back.

With a few minutes to spare before their performance, they check that their instruments are still functional after being dragged and dropped during their escape. They're fine, so they decide to run through the songs to make sure they have all the lyrics down. As they sing, Jake is impressed by how seamlessly their voices blend when they harmonise, especially on the chorus to 'One and Only'.

You are the one and only
Nobody you'd rather be
You are the one and only
Only you can change your destiny . . .

'Miss Bianchi! Mister Jensen!'

Jake and Zoe abruptly stop singing and turn to the doorway. The Fossil stands there, framed against the dim light, every ounce of colour drained from his face.

'Yes, sir?' Jake and Zoe say it in unison.

The Fossil's gaze sharpens as his voice cuts through the air like a blade. 'Why are you singing my song?'

CHAPTER ELEVEN

JAKE stares at The Fossil, stunned. 'I'm sorry. What did you say?'

'I said why are you singing my song?'

'*You* wrote this?'

'Yes. Why are you playing it?'

Zoe's eyes widen in disbelief. She glances at Jake, then back at The Fossil as she processes what he just said: 'Are you – JF Waronika?'

The Fossil reacts as if he has been slapped across the face. 'How do you know that name?' Then his surprise turns to suspicion. 'What are you two up to?'

'Nothing!'

The Fossil's suspicion morphs to anger as he notices the Telecaster, his once pale face now turning a dark shade of pink. 'And where did you find that guitar? That's, that's –'

'Ricky's.'

This time The Fossil looks like he's been punched in the gut. 'How on Earth do you know that name?!'

'He lent it to me. The guitar, I mean.'

Again, The Fossil reacts, but this time he's angry. 'How dare you!'

'The band needs to finish the concert from 1975 so they can pass on to the afterlife.' Jake just blurts it out.

The Fossil stares at him, now furious at being lied to.

Zoe can see he's not buying it. 'They're trapped in Limbo. And have been for fifty years.'

Jake nods in agreement. 'They asked me to look for you, but they didn't know you changed your name after your dad died.'

Zoe adds: 'We went to Alison Place today. One of your old neighbours told us.'

The Fossil's anger only intensifies. 'Why are you doing this?'

Jake shakes his head. 'I realise how out-there it sounds but how could we make it up? *Why* would we make it up?'

'Because I gave you detention.'

'They told me you love Led Zeppelin but you can't stand "Stairway to Heaven". Which, I have to say, is a little weird.'

The Fossil shakes his head, stunned. 'How could you possibly know that?'

'I'll show you.' Jake grabs the guitar, lets his fingers find the strings, raises his pick high, then swings it down and strums the chord of E minor 9.

The Fossil watches the process of summoning the band like a stunned kid who just learned they give out free candy on Halloween. '*What* is going on?'

The three translucent apparitions appear and float towards him. In a flash they transform into JoBeth, Timbo and Ricky – then they see The Fossil and can't believe their ghost eyes.

'JF!' JoBeth rushes over and hugs him tight.

The Fossil hugs her right back, overcome by a moment of emotion he never thought possible. 'You look the same. You look *exactly* the same.'

Then the boys pile in and The Fossil is delighted to see them too. 'Ricky!'

'Hello, mate!'

'Timbo!'

'So good to see you.'

They hug it out – and if you ever wondered if a ghost could cry, well, the answer is yes, they all have tears in their eyes.

After a moment Ricky leans back and looks at his friend. 'You got so old!'

The Fossil laughs. 'I know. I'm positively ancient!'

JoBeth holds The Fossil's face in her hands. 'No, no, no, I can still see you. You're just like I remember.'

The Fossil smiles through his tears. 'I've thought about you guys every day. *Every day*.'

AC/DC
QUEEN

The group hug continues for another moment, then Jake breaks up the reunion. 'Sorry to be the party pooper but we've got a lot to do and we need to be quick. The phantom demon is still out there.'

The Fossil's face darkens. 'Phantom demon? That doesn't sound good.'

'It's not,' Jake says, his tone heavy. 'I'll fill you in later, but right now we need to know the lyrics to the third verse of "One and Only".'

Jo Beth turns to The Fossil, eyes wide with hope. 'Do you remember them?'

The Fossil smiles at her. 'I remember everything.'

The band sighs with relief as The Fossil's walkie-talkie squawks to life. 'Mister Harrington, we need RBJ backstage now.'

The Fossil responds: 'Travelling.'

The Fossil leads the band down a long, shadowy hallway towards the stage area.

The overhead lights flicker weakly, casting long, uneven shadows, while a muted glow seeps through the windows on the left, barely piercing the gloom. As they go, The Fossil recites the forgotten lyrics to the band, who remember them as soon as they hear them –

Bang.

A loud sound reverberates, its source hidden in the darkness ahead.

Everyone freezes.

'Is that the phantom demon?' The Fossil's voice is barely a whisper, his words hanging in the heavy silence like a bad omen.

'Let's hope not,' mutters Jake. Gripping the guitar case like a weapon, he steps to the front of the group and leads them forward. With each step the tension is suffocating, then a dark figure suddenly looms before them –

It's Ms Berman.

Relief floods the group as she grins. 'Great! You're on in five.'

'Thank you, Ms Berman,' says The Fossil. 'I'll take it from here.'

Ms Berman nods and walks on as the band follow The Fossil through a heavy door, which closes with the same loud bang they just heard.

They enter the large backstage area, pass a stack of folding tables and chairs then reach the right side of the stage.

They look out at DJ Hoppy and SnackyBeatz, who scratch and spin their little cotton socks off with a *wiki-wiki* here and a *wiki-wiki* there. Despite their best efforts, the performance ends with a lukewarm smattering of applause from the indifferent audience.

Deflated, the student duo quietly unplug their DJ rig then wheel it off stage with shoulders slumped. As they pass the band, SnackyBeatz mutters to no-one in particular, 'Is it weird to feel the ick about your own gig?'

Once the DJs exit the stage area, Ricky, JoBeth and Timbo's instruments materialise and the band quickly set up. Then the walkie-talkie on The Fossil's hip crackles again: 'Okay, Mister Harrington, we're ready up here.'

JoBeth looks up at The Fossil and asks: 'Are you going to play with us, JF?'

He exhales and is almost embarrassed to say: 'I haven't played guitar since, well – since the fire.'

JoBeth can't believe it. 'But you were so good.'

'I teach it, but playing doesn't bring me any joy. Quite the opposite, actually.'

JoBeth's face clouds over.

'And my arthritis isn't great.' The Fossil painfully flexes his knobbly fingers.

JoBeth doesn't say anything, just takes his hands and holds them in hers.

Jake's disappointed The Fossil can't play with his band but he's hyped he gets a chance to perform in front of a real audience.

Ricky turns to the band, his face grim but determined. 'This is it, guys. *One* shot. We can't stop the phantom demon from coming, but we can keep playing. We finish all three songs. No matter what.'

The others nod with an iron resolve. 'No matter what.' They say it together.

'Good.' Ricky takes a deep breath, then leads them on stage. They move into position, instruments in hand, every muscle taut with anticipation. They're on high alert for the phantom demon and ready to face whatever comes their way.

Jake turns to The Fossil, who stands just off stage. 'If you see anything weird or out of place, or you smell something *really* awful, like just *horrible*, let me know. That'll be the phantom demon.'

The Fossil accepts this with a concerned nod, then says: 'Everybody ready?'

The band all nod. They're ready to rock like their afterlife depends on it.

So, The Fossil triggers his walkie-talkie. 'We're all set down here. Raise the curtain.'

With a swish, the vivid red velour curtain rises and Jake takes in the giant audience before them. Even in the low light he can see that every seat in this auditorium is full. He takes a long, unsteady breath, both petrified and thrilled that he gets to perform for the first time in front of such a big crowd. It almost makes him forget about everything that can go wrong.

Almost.

He must remember to keep his eyes peeled for the phantom demon.

Ricky swaggers up to the microphone with an unblinking bravado. 'Hey everybody, we're here to play you a few rock songs. Let me introduce you to the gang. That's Timbo on drums.' He nods at Timbo, who plays a quick, punchy drum roll. 'That's JoBeth on bass.' He grins at JoBeth, who slaps out a funky rhythm. 'That's Zoe on keys.' He winks at Zoe, who plays a short, sparkling run. 'That's Jake on rhythm guitar.' He points at Jake, who strums a bouncy groove. 'And I'm Ricky. I'll be your lead guitarist and singer for the rest of the evening. We're Ricky & the Blue Jeans and we sure do hope you like our musical stylings!'

The crowd reacts exactly the way you'd want – with enthusiastic anticipation. Then Ricky swings his guitar pick down and strikes the strings of his Stratocaster. The power chord reverberates through the air, heavy and electric, like a thundercloud ready to make it rain rock 'n' roll. 'A one and a two and a one two three four!'

The band launches into the opening riff of 'Hot City Rock'. It's a perfect combination of a song with a rock feel, a slapping bass line and a catchy call-and-response chorus.

Hot!

Hot!

Hot City Rock!

Jake immediately knows the song is fire because within fifteen seconds the audience are up on their feet and dancing their hearts out.

Jake's big revelation is that he has no stage fright. He realises this is the life he's meant to have, playing the kind of music he loves to an audience that wants to dance. He'll do everything in his power to make it happen, and that includes the ten thousand hours of practice. Or twenty thousand if that's what it takes to be as good as the other members of this band. If he was unsure about making that commitment before, he isn't now. He knows it'll be worth it if there's a chance he can do this forever.

The band rips through the first song in just over two and a half minutes, and when they end on a big flourish, the crowd goes bananas. Jake soaks in the waves of affection that radiate from the crowd.

'One down, two to go,' Ricky says with a grin.

Jake glances over at The Fossil, who gives him an enthusiastic thumbs up. He's so old and such a dork, but Jake feels a strange fondness for him now that he actually knows his story, a fondness that would have shocked the Jake from yesterday.

Once the applause dies down, Ricky counts them in for song two and they launch into 'Never Too Late', a pop-rock song with a syncopated bass line and a soaring, melodic chorus.

The audience stays on their feet and keeps dancing. Jake catches Zoe's eye, her face glowing with joy. She's clearly loving this experience. He then can't help but wonder how he'll ever find a bunch of kids who play this well for *his* band.

The song is done and dusted in another two minutes and fifty-three seconds and the crowd's reaction is even bigger and more enthusiastic than before. The band bask in the glory of a good song well rocked.

'Two down, one to go.' Ricky doesn't grin this time as the weight of the moment settles on him. They're *this* close to reaching their goal and yet it could all still fall apart.

There's been no sign of the phantom demon. Relieved, Jake wonders if they managed to scare it off in the gym –

Bang!

The sharp sound rips through the air like a gunshot. Jake spins towards the noise. Through a gap in the heavy, dark curtains at the rear of the stage, he sees that the door to the hallway is now open.

Standing in the doorframe, with shards of the window's shattered glass glittering on the floor behind it, looms a towering, grotesque silhouette.

It advances towards the stage with a slow, deliberate stride, each step reverberating with predatory intent. This creature, this abomination, this *nightmare* come to life, is the living embodiment of Jake's deepest fear. It radiates a darkness so suffocating, a malice so profound, that it is, without question, the most terrifying thing he has ever laid eyes on. In that moment he doesn't wonder if the band will complete its third song, or if his ghost friends will move on to the afterlife.

No.

The only thing he can think about is if he will survive the next three minutes.

CHAPTER TWELVE

A GARGOYLE.

Why did it have to be a *gargoyle*?

Jake would have preferred the phantom demon inhabit pretty much anything else.

It's like it *knows* what scares him.

The gargoyle must be seven feet tall, at least. Being crouched on the side of Nocturne House did a perfect job of concealing its true, terrifying height.

The living rock sculpture creaks and groans as it strides towards the stage with surprising grace. Its claws glint and its stone fangs gleam, ready to tear through anything to stop the band's final song.

Jake's first instinct is to turn and run away as fast as his legs will carry him, leaving this nightmare for someone else to deal with. But that's not who he is – or at least, not who he wants to be. His heart hammers in his chest as he comes to the chilling realisation: only *he* can stand in its way.

The Fossil notices Jake's expression, then inhales the stench with a wince. 'What is *that*?' He turns – and takes in the gigantic gargoyle not twenty metres behind him.

It's such a shock that the old bloke involuntarily takes an unsteady step backwards and stumbles. Jake rushes off stage and catches him before he hits the deck. 'That's the phantom demon?'

Jake nods. 'And I need to deal with it, so you have to play the final song.' As he says it, Jake swings off the Telecaster and holds it out to his music teacher.

The Fossil looks lost as he painfully flexes his knobbly fingers. 'I'm not sure if I can.'

'Then you'll have to dig deep, won't you?' The Fossil hears him and they exchange a grin.

That's exactly what he said to Jake yesterday. With a resolute nod, the music teacher makes his decision and takes the guitar from his student's hand.

The rest of the band turn to see The Fossil slide the guitar strap over his shoulders. They're surprised, then happy. Of course, if they could see the towering gargoyle that strides towards them they wouldn't be smiling, but they can't and that's how Jake wants it. He needs them to focus on one thing: finishing the last song.

As if on cue, Ricky turns back to the still-applauding crowd: 'And for our final song, we'd like to introduce our great friend JF, who will play rhythm guitar!' Then Ricky strums the opening riff of 'One and Only', and the band launch into the tune.

Jake turns to the gargoyle, which is now fifteen metres away. Its weathered, stone body grinds and cracks as it strides towards the stage with sinister purpose. Then it releases a bone-chilling roar that sounds like granite scraping on granite. It's so loud that he wonders if the audience can hear it over the music.

‘I need a weapon.’ Jake looks around and sees the stack of folding chairs. He rushes over and grabs one, surprised by how heavy it is. All the better for what he’s about to use it for.

Jake knows there’s no advantage in waiting for the gargoyle, so he charges the stone colossus then swings the chair like it’s a sledgehammer.

Klang! The metal crashes into the gargoyle’s chest with a thunderous impact. The stone creature staggers backwards but stays on its feet. Jake doesn’t hesitate. Adrenaline surging, he pivots sharply and swings again with all his might.

Klung! The chair connects with the gargoyle’s stomach, forcing it back another step, but still it doesn’t fall. Jake grips the chair tighter and swings once more, but this time aims high.

Kling! The chair glances off the creature’s shoulder and a shower of stone chips fly. A terrible growl escapes the gargoyle and it lunges forward and swipes a massive wing at Jake.

He ducks and feels it slice through the air just above his head. Jake spins around and swings the chair with everything he’s got –

UP

Boom! The gargoyle kicks out a giant foot and nails Jake square in the chest. He flies across the floor like a puck skidding across an air-hockey table – and crashes into a stage flat for the school's upcoming production of *Mean Girls*.

Jake lies in a dazed heap. He's in so much pain he can't move, or even catch his breath. All he can do is lie there and listen to the band, who sound great. The Fossil is doing a bang-up job as Ricky launches into the final verse of the final song:

Against the storm you never bend
Fighting on until the end
Though the odds seem stacked against you
You push forward and break on through
With every step, you prove you belong
When you stand tall and keep marching on . . .

It feels a bit cheesy, but Jake listens to the lyrics The Fossil wrote when he was fifteen years old – and takes inspiration.

He needs to stand tall and keep marching on *right now*. So, with great effort, Jake pulls himself up and finds his feet. It hurts to breathe but he can't worry about a couple of bruised ribs at a time like this.

As Ricky launches into the song's final solo and shreds with a fearless intensity, just the sound of his guitar echoing across the auditorium, Jake turns to see the gargoyle lock its cold, unblinking gaze on the large fuse box mounted on the wall to the right of the stage.

It takes Jake a moment to connect the dots, but when he does, the realisation hits like a freight train.

The creature is going for the power.

If it cuts electricity to the stage, the band won't be able to finish the song – and will be doomed to an eternity trapped in Limbo.

In that instant, clarity strikes Jake. Heart pounding, he takes off towards the gargoyle and shouts to The Fossil as he runs: 'Throw me the guitar!'

The Fossil doesn't hesitate. With his playing duties done for the evening, he steps offstage, swings the Telecaster from his shoulders and launches it through the air towards Jake.

The gargoyle stomps forward, its jagged stone talons glinting beneath the stage lights as it homes in on the fuse box. Then, with a thunderous whoosh, its massive wings unfurl and flap once, propelling it skyward as the gap to the fuse box shrinks rapidly.

Fifteen metres becomes ten becomes five –

Then Jake realises he has a problem.

The Telecaster has been *under* thrown. It's going to smash into the ground before he can get to it. Thinking fast, he drops to his knees and slides across the slick floor like a baseball player stealing home. He stretches out, fingers desperate to grab the plummeting guitar.

Behind him, Ricky strums the final power chord, the sound reverberating like a battle cry.

The gargoyle reaches the fuse box and its claws wrap around its metal lid. With a hideous creak, it wrenches it off and raises its claws to sever the wires inside.

Jake's hand closes around the Telecaster's neck just before it hits the floor. As the gargoyle plunges its claws into the fuse box he spins to his feet and swings the guitar around with all the power he can summon –

Wham. The guitar smashes into the gargoyle's pointy chin with a sickening crack, the force so brutal that it knocks its head clean off. It rockets skyward, its grotesque features frozen in stunned disbelief.

For a long moment, the headless body teeters on the edge of collapse – then crashes backwards like a Jenga tower and shatters into a thousand pieces. A heartbeat later, the head drops to the floor and explodes beside the fallen body.

With a final, triumphant flourish, Ricky finishes his solo. The crowd cheers and the band drink in the adulation. Ricky turns and exchanges a nod with Jake, then smiles at his bandmates. 'I think they like us.'

The others nod. They sure do. But Jake doesn't miss the bittersweet expression on the ghosts' faces. JoBeth is the one to voice what they're thinking: 'Imagine the kind of music we could've made if we'd had the chance.'

Jake has no doubt they would have been legendary. His gaze drops to his hands, which tremble from the adrenaline still pulsing through his body. Then he looks at the shattered remains of the Telecaster on the floor. A wave of nausea washes over him. The thought of destroying such a beautiful instrument feels like sacrilege – even when it was a matter of life and death. Or in his case, life and *afterlife*.

The applause continues and the band take their bow, then The Fossil triggers his walkie-talkie and asks for the curtain to be dropped. It swooshes down as the ripples appear above the stage. In a flash the swirling tunnel is back as the light radiates through it and the air begins to swirl and churn once more.

Jake looks over at Ricky, shocked. 'What's happening? Isn't that the portal to Limbo?'

Zoe is equally surprised. 'Yeah. I thought you guys weren't going back there?'

Ricky shakes his head. 'It's not for us. Now, everyone stand clear.'

As the words leave his mouth, a bloodcurdling screech splits the air. The phantom demon's churning mass of black smoke and shadow erupts from the shattered remains of the gargoyle and is dragged into the portal.

Jake happily waves it goodbye. 'See ya, wouldn't wanna be ya –'

But the phantom demon isn't done just yet.

A writhing tendril of black smoke and shadow whips out of the portal like a striking cobra.

Before Zoe can react, it coils around her waist. Then, with a sickening yank, it pulls her towards the portal.

'What the –?!' She pounds her fists against the shadowy coil, but it only tightens its grip as it drags her towards the swirling void. She is going into the abyss –

Not if Jake can help it.

He doesn't think.

He just moves.

Fast.

He grabs the Telecaster by the neck and with all his might swings down what's left of the guitar's body –

Kerang! It strikes the tendril hard and cuts it clean in half, then smashes into the stage and shatters once more.

Both sections of the tendril fall away and Zoe spins free, then they hiss and shriek as they slither back into the swirling tunnel and disappear. In a flash the portal vanishes and the turbulent air dies away, leaving nothing but an eerie silence.

Zoe catches her breath and nods a thank-you to Jake. He winks a no-worries in return.

Then a single beam of the warmest light shines from above in a soft, radiant stream. It gently fans out and forms the illusion of glowing steps that shimmer like they've been carved from a golden mist.

The Fossil sees it and can only grin. 'That looks suspiciously like a stairway to heaven.'

The band laugh at that then wrap him in a tight hug. There are tears in everyone's eyes but nobody cries. When they pull back they see him as the striking fifteen-year-old boy he once was. 'We'll meet again, JF,' JoBeth whispers, her voice heavy with emotion.

A bittersweet sadness flickers in JF's eyes. 'Can't wait.'

The band turns to the stairway, pausing to hug Zoe and thank her for everything before doing the same with Jake.

Ricky lingers with Jake, who still holds the shattered Telecaster in his hand. 'Sorry about your guitar, man.'

Ricky shrugs. 'You know what's funny? I was going to give it to you.'

'Oh no.' Jake's heart sinks. 'That makes it *sooo* much worse.' He almost wants to weep.

Ricky chuckles softly. 'You'll have one soon enough. Until then, keep practising with what you've got.'

'I will.'

Ricky's expression turns serious. 'I mean it. You're good. Don't waste a second. Time flies.'

Jake nods firmly, even more determined now. 'I know.'

Their eyes meet and a flicker of mutual respect passes between them. They're kindred spirits bound by their shared love of rock. This isn't just a goodbye for Ricky, it's a passing of the torch. He extends his fist. 'All right, let's do this thing. On three.'

Jake, buzzing with excitement, holds out his fist. The others in the band follow. 'One, two, three.'

They bump fists, their voices blending as they say together: 'And the rest is rock 'n' roll history!'

It's joyful and melancholy all at once.

A moment later Jake, Zoe and The Fossil watch the band ascend the glowing stairway. Bathed in the tranquil light, they step into a swirling mist that wraps around them – and then they're gone.

CHAPTER THIRTEEN

As Jake walks towards Nocturne House he glances up at the towering, weathered sandstone edifice and doesn't involuntarily shiver like he used to.

That's because the gargoyle is out of here!

Hallelujah!

Yep, like the missing baby tooth of an extremely creepy infant, that stone horror is no longer perched on the front of the building. It actually took three days before anyone noticed it wasn't there, and its disappearance was blamed on a savage thunderstorm that rolled through the night of the concert, everyone thinking it had been struck by lightning and disintegrated when they found the remnants that Jake, Zoe and The Fossil had surreptitiously moved there from backstage.

So, why is Jake heading into Nocturne House on this fine afternoon? It's not for class. As it turns out, there were quite a few parts on Ricky's Telecaster that weren't destroyed when Jake used it to twice defeat the phantom demon.

He was able to transfer them to Rockenstein and, finally, complete his dream guitar. But once it was built, he needed someone to help him set it up so it actually sounded as good as it looked when he played it.

Turns out there's a guy who's picked up a thing or two over the years, someone who knows guitars pretty well. It seems that being an old fossil does have its perks. You end up knowing all kinds of interesting and valuable stuff. Luckily for Jake, this old fossil is more than happy to pass on that information.

So, after Jake served his detention and cleaned out the attic for calling The Fossil a fossil, Mister Harrington taught him how to set up

Rockenstein, and then offered to give him guitar lessons twice a week.

With each one taking at least two hours, Jake's learning a heap and making good progress towards his ten thousand. And even though there's a fifty-plus-year age gap between teacher and student, they have plenty to talk about because they now share three otherworldly friends.

During their lessons, Mister Harrington enjoys playing guitar for the first time since the fire, and realises it even makes his knobbly fingers feel better. Of course, Jake's skills skyrocket with a real teacher, and just in time because Zoe, still buzzing from their performance at the concert, agrees to start a band with him. They recruit DJ Hoppy and SnackyBeatz, who trade their DJ rig for a drum kit and bass guitar, and soon they're a jamming foursome called Ghost Rock. Mister Harrington even lets them rehearse in the newly cleared-out attic.

So, what's next for these kids and their band?

Well, that, as they say, will be rock 'n' roll history . . .

If you love to be scared . . .

Watch out for more . . .

Dead Scary books . . .